MW01124002

LOVE RUNS TRUE

LOVE RUNS TRUE

•

RACHEL EVANS

AVALON BOOKS
THOMAS BOUREGY AND COMPANY, INC.
401 LAFAYETTE STREET
NEW YORK, NEW YORK 10003

PRINTED IN THE UNITED STATES OF AMERICA
ON ACID-FREE PAPER
BY HADDON CRAFTSMEN, SCRANTON, PENNSYLVANIA

Thanks to the inspiration of my favorite athlete—my husband, Glen.

Chapter One

Susan Silver sprawled on the stair landing midway between the ninth and tenth floors of the office tower. Scattered by her prone body lay a neat leather purse and the contents of an open matching briefcase, several sheets of graph paper, and a tube of Miss Scarlet lipstick that had rolled out when she dropped her load, unable to carry on. Panting and sweaty, Susan was beyond caring that trickles of perspiration were running down her sheer silk blouse. The navy blazer that had seemed so right outside in the early summer morning now clung stiflingly to her delicate body. With great impatience, she stripped the blazer away from her overheated flesh and tossed it carelessly aside, reveling in the coolness of the air-conditioned stairwell, the sweet chill of the linoleum against her.

1

What on earth is happening to me? Susan thought. *Surely this can't be a heart attack!* She fought a rising panic. Her father had succumbed five years ago, and the horrid memories of that time hovered in her consciousness. There had been no warning, and the family was shocked by the death of such an energetic and active man, a man who loved life and instilled in his three daughters a burning drive to achieve any goal they set. Susan had inherited the same small physique and dynamic ambition, a classic Type A whose drive led her to the top ranks at the premier environment control firm in the city—and, perhaps, not so happily, to an early demise.

Recovered somewhat, Susan heaved up on her elbows, determined not to be caught in this undignified position, but that slight movement was all she could manage. She despised feeling helpless, and this loss of self-control, with her body mulishly unresponsive, was not what she'd expected when she'd optimistically bypassed the elevators and chosen instead the unfamiliar stairway.

It can't be a heart attack, Susan insisted to herself in an attempt to calm down. *No nausea, no chest pain, and besides, I'm only twenty-six, far too young to leave this world.* She squeezed her eyes shut and took a deep steadying breath. *Control, I must regain control,* she chanted internally, willing her heart to recover.

Far from stopping, Susan's heart pounded violently

as she waited to expire. Sadly she pictured her mother's distress at losing another loved one. If only she'd had time to get a husband, how much more romantic her funeral would be with a handsome young man there to weep for her under a black umbrella. Both her sisters were married, and lately she'd felt a deep sense of something missing in her life. Now, only weeks after finally dipping tentative toes in the raging seas of mate selection, her life was about to be cut short.

After several moments, when death did not come, Susan opened her eyes and heaved a sad, dramatic sigh that she who loved beauty would have as her last sight a purplish fluorescent ceiling light.

Never again, Susan vowed. *If I live through this I will never sink so low again. I will gain control of my body. I will settle down and start a family.*

The jagged rasp of her breathing echoed off the high ceilings and muffled the sound of approaching footsteps. From the stairway below came a cry of dismay.

''Susan! What's wrong? Are you okay?''

Susan tilted her sleek brown head and focused on the incredible length of Ingrid from consumer relations, six-foot-tall Ingrid, aglow with health, resplendent in a deep turquoise track suit.

''Go away, you jockette,'' Susan said, and gingerly sat up with her legs extended ahead of her to the step below. Not much of a stretch, she thought ruefully.

Ingrid crouched and began to return the loose papers to the briefcase. "Did you fall?" she asked.

"No. I merely collapsed," Susan said with an airy wave of her manicured hand. She grabbed her purse and hugged it to her stomach, still unable to convince her things to propel her upward and onward. "But since I'm not dead I guess I must be fine."

"You don't look fine," Ingrid said, concern in her glance. "You look dreadful."

"Gee, thanks a lot, Ingrid." Susan grimaced. She slowly blew out a lungful of air and smoothed her glossy brown pageboy. "I'm just a bit out of shape, that's all. I'll be quite all right. In a little while. Maybe after a week or so in intensive care."

Ingrid grinned and perched beside her friend on the top stair. Her running shoe kicked out at Susan's stacked-heel oxford loafer, sending the smaller foot into the air. "You ran up ten flights? In those shoes? No wonder you're out of breath."

"Correction," Susan said. "I ran up one flight, walked a few more, then crawled the rest of the way like I was trapped in a nightmare. Oh, Ingrid, how did it come to this? You see before you a twenty-six-year-old shell of her former self. For heaven's sake, I was a badminton star in high school. And a cheerleader. I could do splits!"

"You were just about doing splits on the stairs here," Ingrid said.

"Not funny!" Susan cupped her small chin in her

hand and frowned at the brick wall. "How could I deteriorate to this point in less than a decade? I can't even walk up a measly ten stories. I'm getting old and decrepit. No one will have me."

"Don't tell me you've finally decided to get a life. Are you seeing someone you've forgotten to tell me about?"

Susan noticed a hurt look in her friend's eyes, and quickly corrected her mistaken impression. "No, of course I would tell you. We tell each other everything, don't we, and you know I haven't had a date in two years."

"That's because you always say no when a man asks you out. You prefer to sit at home with your books or stay in the office and trace weather patterns across the globe."

"Sounds good to me. Especially now that I've had this near-death experience. I had great plans to recover my youthful exuberance for sports, but now I'm having second thoughts."

Ingrid lifted a scolding finger. To her, Susan looked like a schoolgirl dressed up in office clothes, a girl who thought she knew it all and refused all advice or guidance. "Now, now, Susan. You know age has nothing to do with it. I'm thirty-six and my body is toned and healthy and in better shape than it's ever been in my entire life. And I've had two kids." To prove her point, Ingrid lifted her turquoise sweatshirt and slapped the firm muscles of her abdomen.

Susan shot her a pained look. "Cut that out, Ingrid. Aren't you supposed to comfort me at this point, instead of showing off? Tell me there's hope for me."

"Why the sudden interest in fitness?" Ingrid asked shrewdly. "The only runs I associate with you are the ones in your stockings."

"Shoot! I paid good money for these," Susan complained with her leg lifted up. Always pretty and polished, she was not about to spend the day in ragged pantyhose.

"Don't worry," Ingrid said. "I have an extra pair in my desk."

"A lot of good your pantyhose would do me. I'm a sweet petite; you're extra tall. On me, yours would sit so high people would think I was out to rob a convenience store." Susan dropped her leg with a thud, deciding to simply remove the stockings and not waste time away from her research lab by going back out to the shops that lined the rows of office towers in downtown Toronto.

"Can you guess why I want to get in shape?" Susan asked with a defiant tip of her chin.

"It's because of your father, isn't it? You don't want to end up like that, and good for you, because now is the time to start," Ingrid said.

Susan frowned in pain at the memory of her father. Did his aggressive and competitive nature contribute to his heart trouble? And if so, was she destined for the same route? Long ago, Susan realized that her del-

icate build and large-eyed face was a magnet for people who felt compelled to protect her, shield her from
the bad things in life. All her life she'd rebelled against
that treatment by being the best she could, the smartest
at school, the lead in the college play, the snappiest
dresser. Small-boned and seeming far younger than
her years, Susan nonetheless ran the research department at the environmental control company like a drill
sergeant. Not only did she love her work, she also felt
that she owed it to her father's memory and to her
mother, who still put in too many hours a week at the
pharmaceutical company.

"No, it's not because of my father. It's the Corporate Sports Challenge weekend next month. I want
to be on the team from Silent Controls."

Ingrid's husky laugh echoed in the stairwell. "For
a minute, I thought you were serious."

Susan squinted her eyes and pursed her Miss Scarlet
lips. "I am deadly serious," she said. "I must be on
that team. Why else would I subject myself to this
brutal stair climb? I hate to sweat, you know that. I
detest oxygen deprivation. But I will sacrifice my in-
tegrity if you'll let me be on the team."

At the sight of Ingrid's stunned face, Susan's determined jaw dropped and she turned big pleading
eyes to her friend. "Please? Pretty please? At least let
me try."

"You realize what you're getting into?" Ingrid
asked, aghast at the idea of this tiny woman climbing

mountains and racing cross-country over rocks and tree roots in some of the most rugged wilderness Canada had to offer. Not to mention the volleyball challenge, where Susan, on tiptoe, might reach the very bottom of the net. Susan was not the outdoor type. With her insignificant body weight, she'd bounce like a rag doll in the bowels of the white-water rafting leg of the challenge.

"The weekend might be ostensibly business related, but the competition is legendary," Ingrid said.

"Ingrid, I'm out of shape physically, but I can do anything I put my mind to. There are six weeks left to get fit. I'm young and healthy. I can do it." Susan glared up at Ingrid. For all her faith in her own abilities, she still had to convince the rest of the world of her strength, even her closest friend. "If others can develop physical fitness, then I certainly can."

Ingrid sat for a minute in silent thought. Susan knew she had her, since Ingrid never won an argument. Susan's superior brain was always one step ahead. Petite she might be, but what Susan lacked in height, she more than made up for in stubborn determination. If Ingrid refused to help, Susan had a backup plan that involved bumping into the company president at his golf club.

"We do need one more woman on the team," Ingrid said warily.

"I know that. I've done my research," Susan said, flexing both her ankles at the same time to ease the tense tendons. The run in her stocking inched higher. "And I also know the president will be there scouting employees for the new vice president position. So I simply must be at the Corporate Challenge weekend. In this company, you schmooze or you lose. I'm through with the ivory-tower life over at Research. It's time I made the decisions, and believe me, I would do a lot better job of it than anyone else."

"But I can't pick you for the team; it's not up to me," Ingrid warned. "Calvin Hart is team captain."

"As I am well aware," Susan said with a secret smile. "You two are good pals, right? Can you put in a good word for me?"

"Why are you smiling like that?" Ingrid asked, suddenly suspicious of Susan's motives. "You can't be interested in Calvin!" Ingrid dropped down on the step and shoved Susan playfully against the railing. Susan, lost in thought, absently rubbed her bruised shoulder, as Ingrid continued. "Calvin Hart is a wolf. He'll eat you alive! He's not a settle-down, raise-a-family guy."

"Nonsense. I've done some preliminary research on Mr. Hart, and Calvin meets all my qualifications."

"What qualifications? You make it sound so scientific."

"It's a logical way to select a potential husband. Find the compatability, then see if the sparks fly. Calvin is intelligent, my number-one priority. He reads. He dresses well. He's smart, handsome, and ambitious and as a lawyer, he can always be gainfully employed, even if he leaves Silent Controls when I take over as president in the years to come.''

''You can't choose a husband based on a résumé,'' Ingrid grumbled. ''What about love and passion? Spontaneity! You are far too controlled, Susan Silver. Anyone who didn't know you would think you were cold.''

''I'm practical,'' Susan said firmly. ''You just get me on that team and I'll handle the rest. If all goes well, I'll kill three birds with one stone. One: Calvin will notice me. Two: Mr. President will be overwhelmed by my extraordinary brain and toned body and announce me as VP. And three: I'll be in shape.''

Silent Controls was a small but growing firm that ran the computerized control for numerous office towers in downtown Toronto, handling everything from waste management to heating and security systems, all in the most modern, environmentally sound way possible. It was a fun place to work, the staff fresh and dynamic. The new VP position was a result of the company's burgeoning client list, and Susan wanted that position with every ounce of her being. She knew how much her research on weather patterns could affect energy savings on a grand scale, but her daily work schedule would not allow enough freedom to pursue her own theories. As VP, she could certainly set up her own research department and free up time to develop her ideas. Of course, eventually Susan planned to be president, but that would have to wait. One methodical step at a time, the same way she had worked her way up to manager—sheer persistence, brains, and a strict adherence to a plan.

Ingrid shook her blond braid. ''How can you want a position that will draw all the company problems?''

''I can deal with problems.''

''And how could you possibly think Calvin Hart would make a good husband?''

''I'm ready to get married. And Calvin is ideal. My preliminary snooping reveals he likes classical music and contemporary novels. Plays squash. No steady girlfriend. And he's quite attractive.''

''Hmm. A steady parade of girlfriends is more like it. Yes, he's attractive. And charming. And also the biggest control freak I've ever met.''

''Me too!'' Susan cried. ''I love to control things. To me, it's not a bad quality. It's a sign of confidence and strength. I'll be married and soon I'll be VP and then I can have children while I finish up my doctorate in environmental studies. Now which sounds better, Dr. Silver, or Dr. Silver-Hart?''

''Silver-Hart sounds like a war medal. And don't rush things. You've got your whole life laid out right up to retirement.''

''I'll never retire,'' Susan quipped. She found a compact in her purse and checked that her lipstick was still in place, bright red on the finely sculpted lips that with her bobbed hair gave her the look of a 1920s starlet. Susan was not vain, but she truly believed that if she looked her best, she would perform her best.

She was surprised to find that she was actually looking forward to getting in shape. The fresh summer weather left her restless and full of daydreams, and for the first time in her life, Susan had been strangely disturbed by the sight of lovers hand in hand on the city sidewalks, of couples snuggled under umbrellas at the outdoor cafés, oblivious to the world around them. A nagging emptiness inside her cried out to be filled, and Susan's busy life was not enough to dull those urgings. Perhaps a rigid exercise regime would offer a new challenge.

Ingrid stood up and leaned against the brick wall, eyeing her friend with a calculating glance. "Even the lipstick doesn't help. You still look like a little kid. I don't think petite women can run a company."

"Oh no? What about Leona Helmsley and her hotel empire? She made millions."

"Was she short?"

"Certainly short-tempered," Susan shot back. "And Coco Chanel. She was absolutely tiny and she became a household name. And don't forget Napoleon."

"I'm happy right where I am, managing consumer relations," Ingrid said. "I don't want any added responsibilities, what with two energetic children at home. It's tough enough as it is, working full time with a family demanding more of me than I can give."

"They'll survive," Susan said drily. "My parents worked constantly and we turned out all right. I plan to have two children and run this company. And buy a dog."

"You can't stand dogs," Ingrid reminded her.

"A cat, then. Two cats, one for each kid. And I'll get my degree."

"Can't be done," Ingrid replied. "All those evenings and weekends. You'll find out about visits to the veterinarian, hockey practice, and piano lessons. Homework. The kids come first for me."

"Please. I think I'm intelligent enough to run a company and raise a family. My mother managed just fine."

"There's more to it than intelligence," Ingrid said. "You'll see. Nannies and housekeepers only go so far."

"I never minded a housekeeper, because my parents were happy and fulfilled. And I am happy and fulfilled too. My sisters are each successfully employed, as a marine biologist and a doctor, with three kids between them. All the Silver girls are special."

"And weird," Ingrid said, earning a rough shove into the wall.

"Well, you're strange too!" Susan joked. "Imagine running up the stairs every day when you don't have to."

"I enjoy being active. Calvin picked me first for the team since he knows how much I like the outdoors."

"No fair!" Susan pouted. "You're a natural athlete. We can't all be jocks like you."

"Oh, yes you can! Anyone can. Susan, you must learn to listen to your body."

"My body tells me to eat popcorn in front of the TV and chocolate for breakfast, in any shape or form."

"No, that's your mind tricking you," Ingrid said. "Junk food is a habit, just like exercise. The more you exercise, the more you'll want to."

"Hah! I just did nine and a half flights of stairs and I never want to exercise again for the rest of my life." *Except I have to,* she thought grimly, determined to make any sacrifice to get on the Challenge team. Susan was used to getting what she wanted, and it wasn't luck that saw her through, but an unwavering plan, well thought out, and a fierce adherence to it. Yet for the first time her insecurity about the inadequacies of her body made the success of the current mission questionable.

Ingrid saw the uncharacteristic self-doubt in Susan's wide-eyed worry and put out a protective hand. "I'll help you, Susan. You've started too much too soon; no wonder you are discouraged. Small advances bring longtime gain. You see," Ingrid continued, warming to her favorite subject, "the lactic acid had built up in your muscle fibers. Give them time to recover. You should alternate weight days with cardio days."

"I don't even know what a cardio day is," Susan

said. "Could you please translate that into plain English?"

Ingrid ruffled Susan's sleek head. "Get yourself a personal trainer," she advised. "Even a couch potato like you can improve in six weeks."

"I loathe the term couch potato."

"Okay, sofa squash then."

"Ingrid, be kind. I'm an intellectual. A PhD candidate. I study, I read, I attend courses to sharpen my mind."

"And eat junk food on the couch."

"I'm the cerebral type," Susan continued, ignoring Ingrid's jibe. "I like cryptic crosswords. I do math puzzles for fun."

"Take that dedication and run with it," Ingrid said. "Literally. Half the trick to being a good athlete is in your mind."

"Then I must be out of my mind," Susan said, rubbing a cramp in her lower calf muscle. "But I can do it. I've already bought a Corporate Challenge weekend wardrobe. A new white bathing suit with no back whatsoever, and high-cut legs. And a pair of those cute little hiking shorts with all the pockets. Calvin won't know what hit him."

As if summoned by enchantment, Calvin Hart came loping around the corner of the stairwell and stopped dead at the sight of Ingrid and that small woman in the hiked-up skirt, the cute one from Research whose name he never quite remembered.

"Hello, ladies." He grinned beneath his mustache, barely breathing hard, his blond hair in perfect waves.

"Calvin, I've told you not to run up stairs in hard shoes," Ingrid scolded, "or you won't have any bones left in your feet by the time you're forty."

"Yes, doctor," Calvin teased, and leaned over to wink at Susan. "Does she boss you around like that too?"

Susan stood up immediately, grateful that she was on the upper step, which still left her well below his shoulder level. His incredibly *broad* shoulder level, she noticed. Her legs, still weak from the exertion, wobbled, and his hand shot out to steady her. At his touch, Susan lifted her luminous blue eyes to his face. Here was a golden opportunity to get his attention, and she had no rigid plans to follow.

"Are you okay?" Calvin asked.

Susan opened and closed her mouth stupidly, cursing herself for being unprepared. The unexpected meeting had thrown off her schedule and she was at a loss how to approach this man.

"She's fine," Ingrid said, with a firm slug at Susan's shoulder. "A simple muscle spasm. A few days' rest and she'll be right back to running her usual three miles a day."

Calvin visibly perked up as he noticed the slenderness of Susan's nipped-in waist, the shapely legs beneath the short skirt. Susan felt his eyes on her legs, and positioned herself so the ugly run was out of sight.

She felt agitated by her lack of control; all her insecurities rushed to the surface as her mind raced to
figure how best to handle the situation. But Susan did
not function well on short notice. Long, slow, logical
progression of thought had always served her well,
and now there was no time to recover. Quickly, she
assumed what she hoped was a confident stance and
plastered a cool smile on her face.

"Three miles!" Calvin exclaimed. "We need a
third woman on our Corporate Challenge team, don't
we Ingrid? A runner, are you?"

Susan stared fixedly at his moustache, more intimidated by the lie he had snapped up. She had a horrible
feeling she was getting in way over her head. In more
ways than one.

"Run!" Ingrid said loudly. "You should see her
run! Susan is a bullet. Small but powerful—you know
the type."

"Of course," Calvin said, with a snap of his fingers.
"Susan Silver from Brains."

"Excuse me?" Susan managed to say.

"Brains is what we call Research," Ingrid said.
"Not to imply that the rest of the departments are any
less intelligent."

"And Consumer Relations is the Fraud Squad,"
Calvin said, earning a hefty punch in the arm from
Ingrid.

"And you guys in Legal are the Crook Nook,"
Ingrid retaliated.

Susan forced a laugh, acutely aware that the easy banter and familiarity between these two was not a part of her own workday, locked away as she was in the tenth-floor office with the research lab attached, where she could check air quality, do water testing, and run her computer in peace and quiet, totally isolated. Susan adored her job. Each day was an adventure into unknown fields, and she frequently got lost for hours, tracking weather systems across the globe. It never occurred to her to venture to the water cooler to shoot the breeze, or join a group for coffee in the lounge. Sometimes her assistant, Nelson, brought in take-out Chinese to share, but that was the extent of her socializing. No wonder no one knew who she was. Well, that was all going to change.

Susan offered her hand in what she hoped was a professional manner and gazed up through her thick lashes, nervous that this crucial first impression was jeopardized by her slow start. She forced herself to concentrate first on the Corporate Challenge team. Romance could wait.

"I'm very glad to be on the team," she said firmly, as if it were already settled. No point letting him mull it over, she decided.

To her surprise, Calvin took her hand in his and raised it to his lips. "Welcome aboard, Susie," he murmured.

Susan winced at the detested nickname, a name for poodles or nursery school nametags. "It's Susan, actually,'' she corrected as he released her hand slowly, leaving behind a lingering warmth.

''Yes!'' Ingrid cried with a well-aimed slug into Susan's bicep. ''What a great team! I'm so glad you're coming. Now the weekend will be so much fun.''

Susan felt a thrill of exhilaration mingled with a nagging dread. Even the fact that Calvin was rabidly taking in every detail of her figure did not assuage her nerves.

''Three men, three women,'' Calvin drawled. ''This could be more fun than I first expected.''

''So who else is coming on the weekend?'' Susan asked.

''Buzz from Sales, and his girlfriend Natalie.''

''The one from Service? Is she the athletic type?''

''So I'm told,'' Calvin said with a scowl. ''Frankly, I'm a bit concerned about her rock-climbing abilities.''

''Rock climbing,'' Susan repeated dully. *And I can't even climb stairs with a railing in an air-conditioned office without severe respiratory damage.*

''Buzz should be fine,'' Calvin continued, ''after all those years in semipro hockey.''

Susan pictured the huge bulk of neckless male who passed her office now and then, an obviously serious athlete.

''Natalie is forward on the women's hockey team,'' Ingrid said. ''She's got great stamina to go with that body.''

They must eat steroids for breakfast, Susan thought bitterly. *Well, I will too, chocolate-covered, of course.*

"And Bob makes six," Calvin said. He threw a casual arm around Susan and squeezed her waist.

Surprisingly, his touch left Susan cold. In spite of his handsome face, and the hard muscles of his arms, and the decidedly masculine scent wafting over her, Susan was unmoved. *Only because I'm nervous,* she told herself, and leaned into the supporting arm.

"So, welcome to the team," Calvin said. "We must do drinks one night to discuss strategy. Or drinks *and* dinner," he amended, looking down with avid interest.

"We'll see," Susan said coyly, confident that her target was at least curious.

"Now take care of those muscles," Calvin said. With a bold wink, he loped up the stairs and through the fire door before Susan could fashion a witty farewell. She slumped as the door slammed above them.

"Oh boy, oh boy. I'm in it now," Susan said.

"Don't sound so gloomy. It's what you wanted."

"But what about the president? I thought he was on the team for sure. Who is this Bob guy?"

"Bob *is* the president."

"You mean Robert P. Simpson, our illustrious and elusive leader? He's 'Bob' now?"

"Sports teams breed familiarity. They play on the same volleyball team. You'll see after one practice, you'll be arms-around-the-neck friends with our president before we even pack our bags for the Challenge."

"Volleyball? Rafting? Why did you have to say I

could run three miles?'' Susan moaned as the enormity of the task ahead hit her.

''You can do it, kid,'' Ingrid said. ''Get a personal trainer. And take the stairs more often. You never know who you'll meet.''

Susan dodged the last punch and climbed wearily up the final set of stairs toward the sanctuary of her office. The enticing scent of warm chocolate hit her nose as soon as she pushed open the door. Nelson, the lab assistant, had brought in his wife's famous home-baked brownies, still warm from the oven. Ignoring the temptation to dive for one, Susan sat down in her comfy leather chair and switched on her monitor, determined to start the first serious training day with no cheating.

It pleased her that things were falling neatly into place. She had finagled her way onto the elite team. And unless she was sorely mistaken, Calvin Hart was intrigued. Susan had expected more fireworks from the first encounter with Calvin, but since even the touch of his hand on her bare arm had failed to stir her, she reluctantly admitted to herself that this relationship was not to be fueled by passion. *I will just have to take the rewards of a more logical, mature relationship,* she decided, and pushed the dissatisfaction out of her thoughts.

''Where's the disk with the molecule breakdown?'' Susan inquired.

''Top right-hand drawer,'' Nelson replied, his

mouth full. He shoved the tray across the antique table that linked the massive desks, an area soon to be covered with Susan's copious notes. Without looking, Susan nonchalantly shoved the tray back. A seductive aroma wafted up and she let a moan of thwarted longing escape the back of her throat.

"Hey, Susan, are you sick or something?" Nelson asked, his glasses glittery under the office lights. "I usually have to hide the brownies just to wrest a few from your voracious grasp."

"I'm in training," Susan announced with great dignity.

Nelson doubled over with laughter and slapped the desk with glee. "You! That's a good one." His laughter subsided enough to let in a huge bite of brownie.

Susan swallowed hard. "Are they low-fat?" she asked soberly.

Nelson inched the tray closer to her desk. "Probably," he said. "My wife wouldn't bake me anything unhealthy, would she? Go on, have one, Susan. They're still warm and the icing is all runny and—"

"Yes!" Susan cried with a mad grab. She bit into the heavenly square and felt a rush of sheer bliss. Nelson's wife sure knew her way around a kitchen.

Her joy was short-lived, rapidly replaced by guilt. "It's 9:05," she said, "and I've already broken training. How come I can control every aspect of my life with steady rationality except for junk food?"

"One brownie won't kill you," Nelson said.

''Not physically. But I must get my head into this training or I won't succeed. Tomorrow I'll start fresh. No more cookies, candies, or chips.''

''Then can I have the dish of jujubes in your desk?'' Nelson asked hopefully.

''No you may not. Jujubes are not junk food. But no nachos and Coke for me. No late-night TV. Regular exercise. Weights, treadmills, the whole nine yards. I'm going to do that Corporate Challenge and do it well. Mark my words, Nelson. I will succeed.''

''They picked you for the team?'' Nelson said incredulously. ''No offense, but do you even own a pair of running shoes?''

''I used to,'' Susan said with a faraway frown.

''How on earth was Miss Twinkie selected for an athletic challenge?''

Susan smiled at his use of her old nickname. ''I was chosen because of my talent—talent for deception, that is. But never mind. Starting today I am a changed woman. And no more Miss Twinkie.''

Out of habit, Susan's hand strayed to the brownie tray, but this time, inspired by her new role of dedicated athlete, she deliberately selected the smallest piece on the tray.

''Starting *tomorrow*,'' she corrected. ''Now where did I put the phone book? I have to find myself a personal trainer.''

Chapter Two

At six in the morning, Feargal Burns stood in front of the billboard in the fitness room and skimmed the list of his scheduled clients. One six-mile run at seven o'clock, Fear read with delight. That was exactly what he felt like doing on this bright and sunny morning. It still thrilled him that he earned his living by engaging in activities he would gladly do for free. He had been blessed with an excess energy that had him continually on the go and a compact, muscular body that never quit. Fear was happier than he'd ever been in his life now that his health club had a steady clientele and he was in a position to hire staff so he could pursue his own fitness goals. Fear liked to consider himself a man of simple pleasures. He liked to wake early and drive his body to the maximum, work at the club, return in the evening to his own little bungalow where his loyal dog waited, and ease into night with a cold beer and a long doze in the hammock. Life was good.

With a proprietary glance, he scanned the training room to make sure all was clean and sparkling before the place opened at six-thirty. Through the plate glass window at the far side, the rosy morning sun dribbled in between the leafy branches of the meadow and left yellow patches on the carpet. The white walls were festooned with hanging ivy and every available space was green with plants, so the members had a sense of the outdoors even as they beavered away inside.

Fear turned back to the board and ran his finger down his duty list. Two fitness tests after the run, new clients who needed a schedule that matched their level. Then an hour of volleyball instruction. Fear dropped his finger. Volleyball? Fear reread the schedule with mounting irritation. His secretary, Madeline, was off her rocker to set this one up. Feargal had no intention of hopping on the volleyball bandwagon at this point in his life.

Now, soccer was a different story. A true sport played in the great outdoors, Fear thought, looking forward to his Tuesday night league where he and his friends toughed it out on the field and then hit their favorite watering hole down by Lake Ontario. All his friends believed Fear had the ideal job—spending every working minute with scantily clad females who clamored for his attention, and nothing Fear said could convince them that he was completely immune to feminine assaults. Once in a while he found a woman he liked and he took her out for a time, but he had yet to meet an earth-shattering dream girl. And certainly the type of woman he preferred was not about to walk into his health club.

In fact, Fear scorned the image-conscious members who showed up in the latest fashions in the most expensive cars and greeted him without removing their ridiculously stylish sunglasses. Volleyball was definitely the latest fad and this appointment could be the tip of the iceberg of popularity. He'd better brush up on his skills.

He traced his finger back to the name booked into that time slot. *Silver, Sue.* Probably another ditsy college girl out to meet boys. A trendoid who hopped from karaoke to line-dancing to volleyball to Hula Hoops. Or with a name like Silver Sue, she might be an exotic dancer who wanted to show off her bod in those skimpy volleyball shorts. Yet, according to the chart, she also wanted a regime set up, so maybe she was serious.

Fear had no control over the wildly diverse clients Get Fit attracted. Not that Feargal would ever compromise his professional status by showing his contempt. He owned the gym, lock, stock, and barbells, and had spent many frustrating years back in Ireland, mindlessly pursuing a dream that was not his own before he woke up one day and decided to gamble on a new life in Canada. It amazed him that someone with his reputation for steadiness and calm could grow so enraged at the memory of those wasted years, although some good did come out of it, he supposed. Most of Fear's friends knew of his time in Ireland, but none knew the final straw that had driven him away. And he planned to keep it that way.

Fear flexed his hard biceps and swung his arms to loosen the honed muscles. Today was going to be a challenge, since his volleyball days were a long way behind him, and he was none too keen on resurrecting his skills. He'd have to to tell Madeline not to book this Silver Sue again without consulting him first.

Madeline's office was no more than a glorified closet, not that she'd ever complained. Fear perched on the chair in front of her desk and looked down with his dark brows furrowed so thickly together they could have been a single line.

"Volleyball?" he questioned with the soft lilt that spoke of an Irish upbringing.

Madeline grinned back at his scowl, secure that those ominously flashing black eyes belonged to a sweetly gentle soul. "Oh, yes. Susan Silver. I felt sorry for her. She's desperate. Poor thing has been rooked into that Corporate Challenge at River Gorge at the end of next month."

Feargal crossed his powerful arms across his chest. By late spring he was always tanned to a dark golden hue from his long runs at all hours of the day and his tendency to spend every waking hour out of doors. Canada suited him. From Toronto to absolute wilderness took less than an hour by car. Indeed, within the city were endless trails and greenbelts stretching from the chic north end down to the harbor, ideal for biking and hiking. During his early morning runs, Fear had spotted muskrats and beaver, quite a few foxes, and more than one deer. Down by the harbor, he could not jog more than a mile without disturbing monumental flocks of Canada geese with downy trails of goslings in their wake. And when he wasn't outside, he was here at Get Fit. Life was very good.

Madeline ignored her boss and picked up her mystery novel. ''I'm at a good spot,'' she said, sure that Fear wouldn't mind.

Fear sighed. Most people would feel intimidated by his dark glare and mighty muscles, but those who knew him were all too aware that his jungle-cat exterior barely covered the pussycat within.

''I mean it, Madeline. Check with me next time,'' Fear grumbled.

''Okay,'' Madeline agreed, not looking up.

''Or give her to Carol. Carol's into all that trendy stuff.''

That got Madeline's attention. ''Carol won't endanger her acrylic nails with a volleyball. And besides, Sue Silver wants a weight routine and she needs a coach for running. Or, as she phrased it, she 'absolutely must learn to run, and fast.' ''

"Is that run fast? Or learn to run fast?"

"Presumably both," Madeline said with a longing glance at her open novel.

"All right. I'll take Silver Sue, but charge her the world and see if we can discourage her."

"Fine. Now don't forget, Fear, you have a haircut booked for three-thirty."

"Cancel it!" he commanded. "I'm going for a bike ride."

"Fear, you look like a rock star with your hair all floppy in your eyes like that. Most unprofessional."

Fear's dusky face broke into a grin. He shook his locks and strummed an imaginary guitar while he bounced around the tiny room. "Now that's what I call a career change. Rock star. I can't play guitar or sing, but that doesn't seem to matter these days."

"I thought all Irishmen could sing," Madeline teased, her pug nose wrinkled.

"No, we just think we can," Fear said, and began a loud and off-key rendition of "Blueberry Hill."

"Oh, no," Madeline broke in and clapped her hands over her ears. "Stop! Or maybe you shouldn't. Look behind you. Your Betty Jean has arrived."

Abruptly, Fear's good mood soured. The Betty Jeans of the world were the one downside of running a health club. Gorgeous, pampered, and aggressive, the lanky blond had targeted Fear as her next victim in love. Fear felt like vanishing out the back door. He had lost count of how many times over the years the same scenario played out, and it always ended with hurt feelings and a canceled membership. More often than not, Fear was immune to feminine wiles, but once in a while, if the loneliness got to him, he allowed himself to get interested in somebody. But he gradually learned from experience that the trouble these relationships caused was not worth it. Fear sighed at the sight of Betty Jean's curvaceous body and wondered if he'd ever feel a spark again. Part of him longed to fall in love again, but not too long ago, in another country, he had been burned by a spark that flared into a blazing inferno. No wonder he was wary of all women. Especially slick, sophisticated beauties like Betty Jean.

"She better not be wearing that ghastly perfume, or I'll let the barbell bounce off that air-filled head," he muttered.

Madeline held up a warning finger like a mother scolding him, although at forty-two she had only ten years on him. "Fear, now you behave yourself. You can't blame the women for falling for your handsome self. Even I had a huge crush on you when I started at Get Fit three years ago, and as a rule I refuse to even consider younger men. For your gorgeous bod I made an exception."

"Madeline, my darling," Fear drawled in a dramatic tone. "If only you'd told me! Is it too late to claim you and elope tonight?"

Madeline laughed at the thought of herself back

when Get Fit was new—so enormously fat and unhappy, a single mother with no work experience and only the ghost of a chance at employment. But Fear had turned her life around. Now sixty pounds lighter, infinitely happier, she was still in love with Fear, but now it was a love based on loyalty and respect.

"You charmer!" Madeline said. "But it won't work. As if you'd ever settle down, with your life so perfect."

Fear was taken aback at her perception of him as an eternal bachelor. It was not how he saw himself, and if his closest friends read him wrong, maybe it was time to open up more. As it was he filled his days with work and his nights with soccer practice and pub nights with his buddies, and outwardly he must seem as if he had the world on a string. Only he knew the disturbing memories that kept him from sleep and drove him to exhaust himself physically day after day. Only he knew how frightened he was to expose himself to the heartbreaking possibilities of love gone wrong.

"But I've told you many times before, Maddy. I'd love to settle down. You know how I love children. I just have to find the right woman."

A loving, sexy, intelligent, athletic earth mother, Fear thought as Madeline regarded him skeptically. A woman who loved dogs and cooking and children and would devote her life to nurturing family life.

"And what kind of woman would that be?" Madeline inquired, her eyebrow cocked in suspicion.

Fear shrugged and picked up the membership leaflet and pretended to be absorbed in the new graphics on the cover. Get Fit now generated so much profit he could afford to pay a professional artist to design the flyers. Such a long way they'd come, Fear mused, since the days when he and Madeline used to spend the evening here while her toddler played on the carpet, eating leftover pizza while they decided whose sketches were less awful than the other's.

"Don't be so fussy, Fear, or you'll end up alone, or maybe that's what you want and won't admit to."

"Am I fussy because I want a woman who will put her family first? The women I meet are so self-centered they couldn't imagine a life without a full-time staff to support them while they go out to work or to work out. Any free time they have, they come here. Where are the children? At day care, still, at six? Home alone?"

Madeline slammed down her fist on the desk. "Get off your high horse, Fear. *I'm* a single mother and I have to work. Am I negligent? I believe that my daughter is well cared for and happy when I return."

Fear knew he'd deeply offended his secretary when he never meant to include her in his tirade. In his life there had been too few loyal friends to take even one for granted. If he lost Madeline, he'd lose his only confidante. Like family, she never allowed him to slip back into the dark depression that had consumed him after his arrival in Canada all those years ago when his life was in splinters.

"I mean the businesswomen who would rather run a corporation than spend time with their kids," he said as he chose a banana from the fruit bowl on the file cabinet and finished it in three big bites.

"I'd like a corporate salary," Madeline quipped.

"Not if it meant sacrificing time with your little one," Fear said, his face wistful. "My own dear mother was there every day for us after school, with homemade cookies and milk, and she listened to us tell about our day."

"And the sun was always shining?" Madeline said, not unkindly.

"In Ireland? Are you crazy?" Fear said, his face sharp once again, his eyes dark as coal. The hard cheekbones gave his face a lean, sinister cast as all softness from the daydream vanished back into the hidden depths of the man. "I might have to go wife-hunting back in Ireland," he said cynically.

"Or back in time," Madeline said sourly, "to bring back a pioneer lady to churn the butter, bake bread, and carry your babies."

"No, I like a modern woman with a few quaint beliefs. Like marriage being forever. And children coming first in a family." The bitterness in his voice drew a pitying look from his secretary, and Fear quickly forced some levity into his voice. "A woman who looks great and cooks better,'' he said lightly. ''Is that so unattainable?''

''A Cindy Crawford/Martha Stewart hybrid?'' Madeline said with a sniff. The banana peel skimmed over her head and she deftly deflected it into the wastepaper basket.

''You weren't listening,'' Fear admonished. ''No career women for me.''

''Fussy!'' Madeline cried.

''Me fussy? What about you, denying the pleasure of your company to that poor young man who hangs around gawking at you, merely because of his youth.''

''He's younger than you are.''

''He is not! And he follows your every move. I have to move his tongue so the clients don't trip on it.''

Fear saw the flush of pleasure creep up his secretary's pale neck. Unable to resist deepening that blush, he leaned over the desk so his face was close to her pretty, snub features. ''Why don't I send him in, give the guy a break,'' he said.

Madeline set her lips firmly and grabbed a pair of scissors from the drawer. Snapping them open and shut, she stood up suddenly. Fear did not like her expression of malevolent glee.

''How would you like that haircut now, from me?'' she said, her eyes dangerously narrowed.

Fear used his powerful legs to propel him out of the office, and kept running past the crowd of women who milled about the weight room hoping for some time with their favorite trainer.

Running late, Susan braked yet again for the lunch-time traffic jam that tangled the downtown core of Toronto. Hungry office workers searched for a restaurant and a parking spot. Susan had heard that the city had more restaurants than any other place worldwide. And right now she believed it. Her stomach grumbled as she saw the sandwich boards laid out along Front Street's wide sidewalks, boasting of gourmet delights and decadent desserts.

At the stoplight she dug into her sports jacket pocket and pulled out a handful of jelly beans. Chewing the candy eased her tension, and she rolled down the window and inhaled a fresh fishy breeze that meant she was near Lake Ontario and the Get Fit premises. Although the light changed, no car moved, and Susan groaned and sat back to wait for the traffic to clear away from the fender-bender up ahead. She hated tardiness in others and was never late herself except in situations she couldn't control. Such as now. And last night. The date with Calvin had been a disaster.

The man was so self-centered he had talked about himself the whole time, about how great an athlete he was and how she should be thankful he had allowed her on the team. At the restaurant, every woman in the place turned her head to admire Calvin Hart, but they didn't have to listen to his continual drone, like

Susan did, trapped across the table. Right away, Calvin disapproved of her choice of pasta in an establishment noted for their steaks and even tried to order for her. Sweet little Susie did not like to be told what to do and stuck to the linguine primavera. By the end of the meal, Susan felt her eyes glaze over with boredom and she idly scanned the menu for a treat to get her over the last few moments she'd ever spend alone with Calvin Hart.

''Put down that dessert menu, Susie. You're in training,'' Calvin snapped.

''There are healthy desserts listed,'' Susan protested. ''Cheese and fruit. And chocolate mousse,'' she cried more loudly so the waitress heard. Calvin was momentarily distracted by his thickly stacked clipboard.

''We get to River Gorge Friday for an orientation party. First volleyball match. Six-mile run Saturday A.M. Afternoon race up the mountain. Sunday is white-water rafting. They supply the helmets.''

Susan ignored his frown of disapproval and tucked into the creamy pudding, happy to salvage some pleasure from the evening. To her, dessert was the best part of any meal. ''Helmets? On a raft? Wouldn't that just make you sink faster?'' Susan mused.

''Have you never been on a river raft before?'' Calvin frowned.

Susan flashed him a Miss Scarlet smile and held out

her fork. "No, I haven't. Want the cherry? It's considered fruit."

"I suppose you want a liqueur with that?" Calvin said sarcastically.

"No. I'll just fire off a Cuban cigar to finish up. Want one?"

Calvin's eyes widened like a gorgeous blue beam. Goodness, he was so dashingly handsome. And intelligent, and so very ambitious. Then why oh why did she not care if she ever clapped eyes on him again?

"Just kidding!" Susan said. At least the vice presidency still looked good, and she would shortly be on the president's candidates list. And the Corporate Challenge weekend was bound to be chock full of successful, intelligent young men who were not hopeless control freaks.

Not wanting to jeopardize her place on the team, Susan stayed outwardly cheerful, even when at the end of the night Calvin dove at her like a duck on a june bug, devouring her mouth in a hungry kiss. A very short kiss, since Susan flew out of the car like the runner she claimed to be and into the apartment lobby before Calvin had time to catch his breath.

Susan ground the Mustang's gears and shot ahead as the lane cleared, skillfully cutting off a taxicab. The outraged honk of the horn didn't faze her one bit. Susan drove with an aggressive confidence that worked most of the time, and the many dings in the car's baby blue paint were most often the other guy's fault. When she spotted Get Fit, Susan jammed her brakes and squealed sharply right into the driveway that ran beside the building.

The health club was cleverly disguised as a row of unobtrusive town houses, with a discreet gold plaque on the door the only identification. The effect was one of quiet elegance and the assurance of quality and professional treatment.

Susan eased the aging Mustang convertible, her father's one concession to lost youth, now in her possession, down the drive and descended a ramp into an underground parking lot.

After a bracing climb of twelve concrete steps, Susan arrived a bit breathless at the rear entrance to Get Fit, which was a spectacular contrast to the understated frontage. Three stories of reflective windows looked down over the sunny harbor past a marina full of bobbing masts and wheeling seagulls. Along an expanse of windowless wall was a mural of silhouettes engaged in various sports activities in a cloud-strewn blue sky. On each level, men and women hoisted weights, huffed away on steppers, or stood in little crowds, talking and laughing.

More than a little intimidated, Susan entered the vast training room that seemed to her as strange and threatening as a torture chamber. It dawned on her that not only was she expected to master these horrific devices, she was also going to have an audience. The gym was abuzz with people. In one corner, an enormous bulk of a man raised barbells the size of her car over his hairless head. In front of the plate glass window, a woman appeared to be trapped on some sort of miniature escalator, doomed to climb forever at a rapid pace until the machine shut off. All over, men and women pushed and pulled levers and pulleys, hefted weights, and pounded on treadmills, all to the thrumming beat of a dance-mix tape.

Boy oh boy, I do not belong here, Susan thought. *I could leave now, get back to the office in time to share a takeout with Nelson and forget this whole insane notion that I have so much as an athletic bone in my pathetic body. Or I could grit my teeth, and do my best, until my best becomes the best, as my father used to say.* After only a moment's hesitation, Susan set her small jaw and moved across the room to a coatrack beside an immense bulletin board plastered with diagrams of people contorted into weird shapes. Reluctantly, she removed the comfortable jacket and stood ill at ease in the skintight bike shorts and matching pink top that the salesgirl had sworn was the height of fashion—the only height Susan was likely to attain.

From the pocket of her jacket, she picked out three more jelly beans and popped one into her mouth, just for the comfort of having something sweet. She was already ravenously hungry. With a pang of regret, Susan pictured Nelson at the antique table feasting on tacos and salsa, classical music wafting from his portable CD player. Get Fit was too brightly lit and noisy.

She turned from the happy din on the floor and noticed her name jump out from a list on the board.

Noon:	Silver Sue	Test	Fear B.
		Weights	Fear
		Volleyball	Fear

Susan swallowed hard. Nervous, maybe. On edge, definitely. But fear? Fear was a little strong to describe her present state. Perhaps fear would descend, with its fierce irrational claws dug in, during the Corporate Challenge, when she was snagged on the edge of a cliff or hurtling headfirst toward a foamy river rock. But here, in the unfamiliar confines of Get Fit, Susan decided she was merely on edge.

"Silver Sue," barked a deep, lilting voice.

Susan jumped a foot and whirled so fast her shiny bob swirled out behind her in a mahogany fan. The first connecting glance at the man stuck so she couldn't look away from the darkest, softest, most liquid eyes she had ever seen on a man—eyes not entirely black, but alive with myriad hues of nightshades that moved and flickered as she stared, dumbstruck, floating on the soothing motions of those shadows.

A small hum of a word came out of her mouth, short and low, a sound that even to her ears sounded terse and haughty. As if she could be haughty when she was under the spell of those eyes! The lashes, she noticed, were so thick they tangled into a pattern of dark lace, and his bushy eyebrows almost met in the middle of his swarthy face. *Get a grip, Susan,* she admonished herself. Slowly Susan lowered her chin, her eyes still locked onto that intense gaze so her own eyes tilted up. He was not smiling. What on earth did he think of her, Susan wondered, and began to tremble from the strain of holding her own in such a strange and stimulating situation.

Fear Burns forgot the reason for his hostility as he looked down at the petite and vulnerable woman who was dressed like every other woman in Get Fit, yet who resembled no earthly creature he had ever encountered. He had never seen such large glittery eyes on any human, so full of hope and dread, agleam with intelligence and a disturbing spark of sensuality. Mutely, Fear returned her regard, aware of an odd feeling in his gut. He opened his mouth, hoping that his newly blank mind would send him some form of basic greeting.

''Hi,'' he said and clamped his mouth shut again. *Brilliant,* he thought disparagingly. *Do I have to sound so much like a dumb jock? Now think of something else,* he urged his frozen brain. *Go on! Take charge,* he commanded his whirling thoughts, who refused to obey.

''Hi,'' Susan said back.

Fear's hand shot up and ruffled his already messy

hair into a shaggy black mass, a teenage habit long since buried only to resurface now. Seconds ticked by.

Gradually the lights and sounds from the rest of the world returned and Fear's face folded into its familiar scowl. "Come with me," he said gruffly.

After a moment of stunned silence, Fear saw the woman's pointed chin tilt up. "Do I know you?" she said haughtily.

"I'm Feargal Burns. Your personal trainer," Fear said.

"Oh, I get it! Feargal is Fear! I saw the bulletin board and I thought I was in for trouble here at Get Fit."

Her smile vanquished all traces of haughtiness, her teeth so white against the bright red lipstick. Fear's immediate sense was one of doom. This woman was different. He was enchanted by the confident voice emanating from that delicate face, a voice with a faint rasp, as if this dolled-up street urchin had been yelling to friends on darkened streets.

"Feargal is an unusual name," Susan said.

"Common enough in Ireland," Fear said. His head tipped down to catch her words, an unusual posture for Fear, who was strongly built but compact and not used to towering over anybody. This Silver Sue was so fine-boned and alarmingly pale, as if the light of day never met her beautiful form.

Abruptly it occurred to Fear that Susan was a client, one he had to mold into some semblance of an athlete.

The challenge was extraordinary, but the task, with all the hours together it entailed, no longer bothered him.

Susan felt a chill and rubbed her bare arms.

"Come with me and we'll do a basic fitness test," Fear said. Instead of leading, he indicated with a sweep of his arm a narrow carpeted path that led to a private room beyond the chaos of the main club.

In the room, she turned to face him, her face tilted trustingly up, her luminous eyes wide with barely hidden terror. "Let's begin then, shall we?" Susan said. "What do I do first? Boy oh boy, I'm ready for this."

To Fear she seemed as sweet as a kitten in a thunderstorm, mewing boldly to scare away the creatures of the night. "We'll get you to answer a few questions and do some body measurements."

On a neatly organized tabletop, Fear assembled a tape measure, a few typed forms, and a huge pair of metal tongs. He saw Susan's look of dismay and was struck again by how vulnerable she seemed. Those bowed lips and the bobbed hair, the lined, shimmery eyes—she was so like a silent-movie heroine trapped with a nasty villain leering down at her quivering body. But Fear didn't want to be the villain. He wanted to be the hero.

He grinned with what he hoped was good-natured friendliness, with no outward trace of the attraction he felt stir as he stood near her warm, vanilla-scented body.

"I'll take care of you, Silver Sue," he said softly.

Still facing her, unable to look away, Fear backed into the door and leaned on it till it closed with a slam. Deftly, he reached behind him and slid the bolt firmly shut.

Chapter Three

A line of deep heat crisscrossed Susan's body as she faced the man who was now alone with her in the confines of the small test room. Fear's sullen face showed no trace of pleasure as he fastidiously studied her body. Embarrassed, she looked up and saw that Fear's intense scrutiny had shifted now to her face.

"It's okay, Silver Sue," Fear said gently. "I'm not going to hurt you."

"I know that," Susan said doubtfully. "I'm a bit on edge because I've never done this before. I like to have a basic grasp of what I'm getting into, and today I don't have a clue."

"I've done it hundreds of times, so leave the details to me."

Fear stacked a few sheets on the table. He turned

from his task and caught her admiring his broad shoulders, yet his expression remained stern. Susan couldn't believe he hadn't noticed his effect on her—the shallowness of her breath, the pounding heart whenever he approached. Maybe he put it down to a bad attack of nerves. Or more likely, Susan thought ruefully, he had hordes of women swooning at his feet every day of the week. Women with abdomens like brick walls and curves galore. Women who could run three miles while making business deals on a cell phone.

"First of all, some ground rules," Fear said briskly.

"Yes, give me some guidance," Susan replied. "Am I dressed all right? I had no idea what to wear for a fitness evaluation."

"You're dressed well. But you're tardy."

Susan responded with a tight-lipped grimace. "I'm sorry I was late. It wasn't my fault. There was this decrepit Toronto cab in front of me and Front Street is down to one lane, so I had to really hit the gas to blow past him at the light, or I'd be even later. But trust me, it won't happen again. I'm usually obsessively punctual."

Fear nodded and took her wrist in his hands to check her pulse rate. Susan heard his sharp intake of breath and looked down to see her palm tinged green by the clutch of jelly beans she'd held in her palm during the drive.

"It's not a disease," she reassured him. "I'm a bit of a junk food addict, especially jelly beans. I guess you could say you caught me green-handed! I always save the green jellies for last.'' Only when the words came out did Susan realize how childlike they sounded. Fear was bound to get the wrong impression.

Fear suppressed a smile. ''If you're serious about getting fit, there'll be no more junk food at least for the next few weeks, preferably for the rest of your life.''

''Jelly beans are not junk food,'' Susan pronounced. ''Gelatin is actually good for your fingernails. I am certainly not giving up jelly beans.''

Fear tilted his head and the rough waves of his hair fell over his forehead. ''Let's get one thing straight right now, Silver Sue. You've hired me, but that does not make you the boss. You pay the money, but I am the boss. Are you going to have trouble accepting that?''

Susan blinked her eyes rapidly, searching for the right words to explain the difficulty she faced in accepting any outside control whatsoever. Her resistance to any sort of attempt to sway her from her steadfast opinions was so developed it hurt to give in. But now, in a twisted sort of way, Susan wanted to be guided. In the deepest recesses of her mind, so buried she was unable to admit it to herself, she was tired of the constant strain of decisions and schemes that she made entirely alone. Now Fear Burns, his bushy brows raised in question, was commanding her to let him take over this aspect of her life.

"Susan, are you listening? Don't daydream on my time. Do you understand that I make all the decisions, all the rules, and you either agree to obey them now, or find another personal trainer?"

"I'll obey the rules," Susan said. In the back of her mind a similar phrase thrummed up: *love, honor, and obey.*

"You will obey my rules," Fear said firmly. "Good. Now a few basic questions." He raised a massive thigh and set the sheet on it for a writing platform. With his weight unbalanced on one leg, the muscle in his calf grew and hardened like a submerged brick.

"Height?" he asked, pen in hand.

"Five-feet-two. All right, not quite. More like five-foot-one and a half. Almost."

"Weight?" Fear asked, his mouth twisted in a quirky smile.

"One hundred and five. Or so, depending on the scales."

"Over eighteen?"

"Oh, now come on, I look older than that, for heaven's sake. Oh," Susan said as she saw his eyes crinkle with delight. "You're joking."

"Over forty?" Fear said, laughing aloud now.

"I'm twenty-seven."

"Twenty-seven," Fear repeated.

"Almost," Susan said.

"Occupation?"

"I'm a research scientist. At an environmental firm."

Fear's interest sharpened. "Really?"

"Yes, really," Susan replied huffily. "Actually I'm manager of research and development. Why is that so hard to believe?"

"It's not hard to believe," Fear said mildly.

"Because I'm female? Because I'm short? I don't like the astonishment I see in people's faces when I simply state what I do."

"I'm impressed, that's all," Fear said. "We don't get many scientists in here. I'm interested in environmental research."

"Yes, it's a fascinating field. I'm a meteorologist and I'm studying molecular biology at present."

"You manage a company and still go to school? I'm even more impressed."

Susan instantly clammed up. Behind his pleasant expression, she noticed an unmistakable gleam of amusement. *He probably thinks I'm a geek now,* she thought, surprised at how unhappy this made her. Tonight, he'd be quaffing beer with his jock buddies at the local sports bar and get a few laughs at her expense.

Susan raised her chin and clasped her hands behind her back, ready for Fear's next question.

"Any allergies or health problems? No? Any major operations?"

"I got my ears pierced when I was thirteen," Susan said.

"Do you smoke, or drink more than one or two ounces a day?" Fear said.

"No. Unless you mean Coke. I love my Coke, but I suppose you'll forbid me that pleasure as well."

"There will be other pleasures to compensate," Fear said. After a pointed pause, he unbalanced his leg and stood beside her. In the reflecting mirror, Susan saw that if she tilted her head to one side, his shoulder was at the ideal level to receive it. If he were to encircle her waist, they could stroll forever without discomfort. With her slight figure and his compact body, Fear and Susan were a perfect fit.

"You do seem very healthy," Fear said to her reflection.

"Actually, I'm as healthy as an ox. I eat fruits and vegetables along with the pizza and tacos. And I get a lot of sleep. I'm not into the nightlife. I'd rather curl up with a good book, and then I get so sleepy I end up putting the light out." Susan bit her tongue. Why did every piece of information she offered have to reinforce her science-nerd status? "But I drink wine coolers. A lot! You should see me in the summer. One after the other," Susan said hurriedly. "And I stay up late when I go to a party. Very late, I might add."

"I like to be in bed early too," Fear said.

In that instant, Susan could have sworn that Fear leaned closer to her, and she responded instinctively by softening her own tense muscles, so that she edged closer too. He seemed to inhale a slow breath, or maybe it was a sigh, Susan thought, a weary sigh for the task ahead.

''That's it for the questions,'' Fear said, and slapped the sheet against his palm. ''So we'll move right on to the fun stuff. And don't be nervous. It will skew the results.''

''Is that an order?'' Susan said, more casually than she felt. Butterflies escaped her stomach and brushed agitated wings against her heart. It was the same sensation she carried into every exam she'd ever written and excelled at, but this time it was tinged with a different quality that excited and terrified her.

Fear stood so uncomfortably close that Sue could smell warm skin mingled with the fragrance of sunshine-y clothes, an outdoor smell that was instantly appealing.

''Yes. Now tell me what you want from me,'' Fear said.

In the ensuing clap of silence, Susan's mind raced with delicious possibilities before she forced herself to put the brakes on. Ashamed and startled at her uncharacteristically flirtatious frame of mind, Susan decided last night's disappointing date combined with her feverish work schedule and the unfamiliar physical demands she'd placed on her body had shifted her usual unwavering dedication to logical thought. And, she marveled, it was not an altogether unpleasant shift.

"I want you to make me physically fit."

"Why?"

"So I can run three miles for the company team at the Corporate Challenge."

"Why?"

"For a lot of reasons! Is this interrogation necessary?"

Fear reached out and placed a calming hand on her narrow shoulder. The action had the opposite effect on Susan, who jumped as if she'd been shot with an electric current.

"You are a bundle of nerves. Now relax, and that's an order. I'm in control now," Fear reminded her.

Susan's breath quickened. "I want to run because I can't sit around and do nothing for the rest of my life. I don't want to die young of a heart attack. And I want on the Corporate Challenge team because the president will be there scouting new talent for the vice presidency position, which I desperately want. And deserve."

Susan saw a wave of anger pass over Fear's black eyes, a ripple of disapproval that was gone as fast as it had appeared. "Do you always get what you want, Silver Sue?" he said.

"If I want it badly enough, then yes, I always do," Susan said.

"What if you get what you want and then realize you don't want that at all?"

Susan heard the bitter note in Fear's tone and instinctively knew that there was a lifetime of experience behind that simple statement. For the first time, Susan saw beyond the incredible body into the whole man, and her curiosity was piqued. What had Fear gained and lost; what had life handed him that gave him that inner core of strength? And how could such an obviously sensitive man be happy employed in the shallow capacity of a sports trainer? Gorgeous he might be, but not the cerebral type, Susan decided. Her steely inner voice warned her away from the growing attraction to Fear Burns.

Even now, as she felt the warmth where his hand had been, she knew that no matter how strong the attraction, she must not get involved with a dumb jock. Her carefully laid-out life would be turned into a shambles. Then she'd be hopelessly in love with the wrong man. That must never happen, Susan thought. Best stick to her logic when picking a mate and ignore the irrational calls of nature that left couples irredeemably mismatched. The hairdresser and the doctor. The garage mechanic with the ad executive. The jock and the scientist. And the inevitable divorce and suffering that followed.

''So I'm to transform you into Wonder Woman so the top brass will be so bedazzled they'll offer you a promotion,'' Fear said, rifling in the top drawer of a metal desk.

''That is correct,'' Susan said, her voice cooler now.

''Get up on the platform,'' Fear said, indicating a

small wooden box in the center of the room. A mirror stretched floor to ceiling along the back wall and the overhead lights flickered dimly. Even up on the step, Susan was only a bit taller than Fear. When he wrapped a measuring tape around her torso, she sucked in her already narrow waist. In the mirror, she saw Fear's face, the tangly lashes lowered against the hard cheekbones, serious in repose.

She could sense how careful he was to maintain propriety, but even so, the heat of his fingers radiated against her rib cage when he took the final reading. The faint caress, all the more powerful for its subtlety, was repeated when he circled the tape over her hips. To him, it was probably all business, since he'd done this exact routine hundreds of times with many female clients, but to Susan the charge of energy was almost unbearable. She closed her eyes and tilted her face to the ceiling.

When she next opened them, the tape was gone, to be replaced by an enormous pair of calipers. Susan's black-lined eyes opened even wider, like a silent-movie star tied to the railway tracks, and she shied away from his approach.

Fear assumed a kindly if exasperated expression. "This won't hurt, Silver Sue. Don't look like a deer caught in the headlights," he said lightly.

Susan's bowed lips pressed together and she tried to unclench her fists. She forced an airy laugh. "Fine, just as long as those stay there and I stay here,'' she said.

Fear laughed and clicked the calipers like castanets. ''This is to seek out and measure body fat.''

''Fat!'' Susan said scornfully. ''Not on *my* body. I may not be in shape, but I am very fastidious about— whoa!'' she cried as the metal tongs fastened onto the crease of flesh below her left shoulder blade.

''Found some,'' Fear said smugly. ''And here,'' he continued, as the metal assaulted her waist, and then her spandexed belly.

Seeing her acute embarrassment, Fear had the grace to stop smiling. ''You're a woman, Susan. You are gracefully slender, true, but womanly, and that means fat deposits. That's normal. We'll change some of it into muscle, but I wouldn't want you to lose those soft curves. You're beautiful.''

Susan heard the sincerity in his voice and her eyes met his for a long tranquil moment, a totally unconscious instant of honest evaluation. Fear pulled back first.

''Don't worry,'' he said with a grin. ''I'll whip you into shape.''

In spite of her worries, Susan responded to his smile with a dazzling one of her own. ''I don't like your choice of words, sir,'' she said lightly.

''Whip is just an expression. As you'll discover, I do have a secret weapon for the runners I train. But it's not a whip.''

Susan pursed her red lips and allowed herself a quick scan of Fear's agile muscles and strong limbs. She hopped down from the platform and rubbed her cold hands together. "So what is your secret weapon?"

"It's Eire. You'll find out."

"As in air you breathe?"

"Now, it wouldn't be a secret if I told you," Fear said.

Susan sprang lightly on her new shoes, energized by the almost tangible charge in the air, as if a violent thunderstorm approached even as the sun shone down.

"So shall I book the next appointment?" she asked.

Fear shook his head, a wicked grin on his swarthy face. "You can't possibly think I've finished with you," he said. "Silver Sue, I've only just begun."

An hour later, after Fear had walked a shell-shocked Susan to her car, he bounced into Madeline's office.

"Book me a haircut, Madeline," he said. "And slot Susan into the earliest Friday-morning space. Do you think my shirt is too ragged? I ought to get some new workout clothes."

Madeline looked up from her computer monitor, astonished by the abrupt change in his manner. "You actually want a haircut? What's come over you?" she said with a shrewdly intent squint.

Fear drew his bushy brows together. "Is there something wrong with a man taking pride in his appearance? I'm thirty-two years old, not a teenager afraid of a visit to the barber. Oh, and maybe you'd better put Susan Silver in regularly over the next month. Mondays, Wednesdays at noon, Friday morning.''

Madeline slammed down her glasses and stood up to lean across the desk. ''Okay, that's the tip-off. Since when have you ever concerned yourself with a client's booking? You've got a crush, don't you? On that little doll with the pink bike shorts.''

''Don't be ridiculous, Madeline,'' Fear said with a dark scowl. ''I'm interested in the challenge of training her. She's not very strong physically but I can tell her mind is powerful. I'm curious to see how she'll work out, that's all. It's a strictly professional curiosity.''

Madeline's pitying look infuriated Fear. She was a great secretary, but it was eerie the way she could see into his mind.

''Don't look like that, Maddy, or I'll have to fire you.''

''You can't fire me. Get Fit would shrivel up and die. Now Fear, you haven't had a serious date in the three years I've been here. If you find this woman attractive, then do what most normal men do and ask her out. Live a little.''

''You're a fine one to give advice. Every man who asks you out gets the cold shoulder.''

''One man has asked me out in the last year and he

was barely more than a boy. I don't date younger men.''

"And I don't date career women," Fear snapped. He picked up an apple from the fruit bowl, eyed it balefully, and put it back with bruising harshness.

"So that's it," Madeline said. "Fear, darling, just because your ex-wife chose a career over a family life is no reason to condemn every working female."

Fear's face closed in as it always did when he spoke of his years back in Ireland. Even now, it still hurt to remember. "That was a long time ago. I'm happy the way I am, Maddy. I won't rock the boat. But I still need a haircut."

With a smile he didn't feel like faking, he left Madeline's office well aware that she alone knew the dark days in his past that had brought him overseas. One long rainy afternoon in the early days when Get Fit was a hole in the wall, they'd shared a bottle of wine and the secret heartaches that had led them to this point. Madeline had held her own through two divorces, and helped Fear get through his own marriage breakup.

Fear strode across the fitness floor, ignoring the chorus of greeting from the throng of clients, and went straight to the most challenging machine in the club, a ten-foot-high bar nicknamed the Gut-buster. In one fell swoop Fear leaped up like a panther after prey and grabbed the bar, rising up on powerful forearms, over and over until his muscles trembled and his skin was filmed with sweat.

He couldn't fall for Susan Silver. But it was too late; he already had. What had been infatuation at first sight of the dainty figure, the lusciously bowed lips, had turned into an intrigue that bordered on obsession. Fear had gritted his teeth to stop from probing her about every aspect of her life. Even now, as he worked himself into exhaustion, Susan's small triangular face with the pugnacious tilt to her jaw was in his mind's eye. With a jolt, Fear dropped to the floor and moved immediately to the next apparatus, a chest press loaded with weights the size of hubcaps.

But I can't fall in love with her, he thought with an agonized groan. The course had been set and he was as in control as a feather in the wind. His teeth clenched, his pecs bulging with mighty effort, Fear remembered his ex-wife Mary back in Ireland, another petite beauty who'd betrayed him by choosing a career over a husband and family. They'd had it all, two of the most celebrated plastic surgeons in the UK, with their own clinic, making money hand over fist. But as soon as Fear wanted a baby, as soon as he'd decided that something was missing in his outwardly perfect life, Mary informed him that she was not about to give up her world, not even when Fear assured her that he would take equal time out for child-rearing.

Fear desperately loved children and wanted several. When he saw what money and ambition had done to his childhood sweetheart, he'd abandoned Ireland and his medical career. Deciding to follow his natural proclivities, he'd started out alone in a new world. The result was Get Fit, which was wildly more successful than he'd ever imagined. It seemed to Fear that he was destined to make money, when all he ever wanted was a family and an old-fashioned wife to look after him. A wife who looked exactly like Susan Silver, and who talked like her.

But how could a research scientist be satisfied with a domestic life? It was the same old story. Fear was hopelessly drawn to a woman with brains as well as beauty, but he couldn't bear the notion of the mother of his children not being content as a devoted housewife. This meteorological research was a passion for Susan; he could see that by the light in her eyes as she spoke of it, a calling not easily abandoned for the sake of bearing and raising children. Fear grimaced again, thinking of the warm vanilla scent of her, as if she'd been baking cookies all morning instead of consulting satellite images.

"Ah, excuse me," piped a lovely feminine voice.

Fear turned blank eyes to a stunning redhead in a very tiny outfit.

"If you're through with the machine," she said hesitantly.

Fear stood up, still lost in vivid images of Susan, and absently ran his fingers through his hair. For a moment, the redhead met his eyes with a look of clear invitation. Oddly enough, the gorgeous woman, like legions of women before her, left Fear cold. All he could think about was the fine bones that made up Silver Sue's slight form, her silent-movie-star face, and the two interminable days between now and Friday, when he'd be with her again.

"Sorry, darling," Fear said in the musical Irish lilt that Canadian women, for some odd reason, found irresistibly appealing. "I was lost in thought."

"And what does a man like you think about?" the woman purred, arching her back close to Fear's sweaty body. Fear didn't even notice.

"Environmental research," he said with a faraway smile.

Chapter Four

Susan lay flat on her back on the weight bench, trembling, her clothes practically dripping with sweat. Her bangs stuck damply to her forehead, dark and lank, and her breath came in jagged sighs.

It was hot, far too hot and steamy, and she'd lost all track of time. Never before had she felt this way, so light-headed and weak, almost dizzy from the depth of sensations rushing over her. Fear loomed above her, his dark face sober, and she closed her eyes to blot him out.

"I can't," she gasped.

"Yes. Yes, Susan, you can," he said.

"No," she breathed. "Fear, please! Please don't make me."

"Susan. I insist."

Angrily, Susan's eyes flew open and she gritted her teeth and forced her meager arms to summon every last ounce of strength. Slowly, painfully, the heavy bar inched up even as her arms began to grow numb with the effort. Just when she thought she could no longer carry on, that her arms were about to buckle, Fear's strong hand circled the bar and helped her ease the weight back to its resting place in the slots above the bench.

Susan's ragged breathing sounded overly loud as she let herself droop over the bench, totally limp, while the blood rushed back to her poor overworked muscles. It was only her second weight room session with Fear and she was still recuperating from the last assault. The man was a tyrant, she decided. He simply adored barking out commands, and not only did he push her beyond her limits, he also seemed to enjoy the sight of her suffering. Even now as she struggled to sit up, he stared down with the big wicked grin of a pirate nudging his victim off the gangplank.

"Tell me, Fear, what is so funny?" Susan grumbled from her prone position.

"Am I laughing?" Fear asked innocently. He held out a hand and dragged her up to a sitting position. "Here, drink some of this and you'll feel like a million bucks in a few minutes."

Susan grabbed the bottled water and drank gratefully. "I've never felt worse in my life," she said wearily. "Or looked worse, I'm sure."

"I personally like a woman who can work up a good sweat," Fear said casually, "so you better get used to it."

Susan quickly averted her eyes and finished the entire bottle of water in one gulp. Fear had a way of taking the simplest sentence and twisting it into something more. Or perhaps it was all in her mind. Maybe he made innocuous statements and it was her own irrational attraction to him that made him appear flirtatious. Not that he needed any help. The man's body was so well honed and graceful, he seemed to be the epitome of masculinity. And his eyes, those black intense eyes. Susan was sure Fear found her attractive as well. Such a strong pull couldn't be all one-sided, could it? And when she was with him, Fear turned his undivided attention her way, no matter how many clients clamored for his time. On the run through the back streets the day before, Fear had asked so many questions about her personal life, Susan had begun to suspect that he was going to ask her out. But he'd said good-bye casually. Even though Susan would have declined a date, she had felt an odd sense of disappointment as they parted. Of course, now after thinking about it, the whole idea of a relationship with a man like Fear Burns was ridiculous. Susan was an intellectual, an ambitious career woman who needed a dynamic, intelligent man in her life. An intellectual equal. Not a sports fanatic who probably didn't even own a tie. They were from such different worlds they'd have nothing to talk about. Susan knew nothing about sports or sports teams and Fear had probably never been to a cocktail party, let alone an art gallery. And yet, something about the man was intriguing.

Susan looked up into Fear's face and saw his smile was gone. With the new short haircut, his cheekbones seemed harder and gave his face a sharp, almost dangerous look.

''Are you all right?'' he asked.

Susan nodded, unable to look away from his dark gaze.

''Good. Are you free tomorrow morning?'' he asked offhandedly. He tossed her a towel and she stood and draped it over her neck.

''But I thought we'd agreed on three times a week to train,'' Susan said, her head cocked inquisitively.

''Yes, but remember, I want you to get some 'Eire time.' ''

''Oh, yes,'' Susan said, her eyes wide.

''So how about a run and then breakfast? I know a terrific pancake house where they serve eleven kinds of syrup.''

''Even chocolate?'' Susan said. She was feeling better already.

''Even chocolate, Silver Sue,'' Fear said. ''And if you're a good girl I'll let you pour that chocolate syrup all over what you Canadians call the tall stack.''

''It's a deal,'' Susan said, and headed off to the

luxurious ladies' room, where a shower and a fragrant sauna would fix her up for the rest of the day.

Back in the cocoon of her office, Susan took the crystal dish of jujubes from the top drawer of her desk and set it down in the usual spot beside her keyboard. The bright colors beckoned her. The sweet scent of candy wafted up. Yet Susan, with great strength of will, resisted the temptation to immediately pop one into her mouth. Determined to change her bad habits, Susan forced herself to trace the edge of the fluted dish with one finger while she counted slowly to ten.

"I can do it," she said under her breath. "I can!"

Hurriedly, she shoved the candy back into the drawer. No junk food. That, to her, was the hardest part of this training schedule—not the weights, or the working out, or even the running. In fact, running with Fear by her side was more fun than she'd ever imagined. *Whoa!* Susan warned herself. *I will not think about Feargal Burns.*

The computer screen beeped at her when she rested her elbow on the keyboard, but Susan didn't respond. Chin in hand, she decided that it was fine to admire the man—any woman would—but she had to stop fantasizing about a relationship with him. No, it simply wouldn't do to let Feargal Burns into her life, not now, when her career was flourishing.

She was on the verge of attaining real power in her job, since the president was bound to notice her now that she was on the Corporate Challenge team. *I've got it all,* Susan thought smugly. *Beauty, brains, and body, or almost a body,* she conceded. Who said you couldn't have it all? With careful planning and unswerving dedication to a schedule, Susan was going to get the life she deserved. No complications with a man like Fear. She'd just have to ignore the attraction she felt. Susan clicked onto a computer icon and a spreadsheet fanned out across the screen. *My own creation, with data that could contribute to energy conservation,* Susan thought proudly, and was soon lost in her work.

A knock at the door jarred her back to reality.

"Go away!" she called, her hoarse voice loud and vibrant.

"A moment of your time, Susan."

Susan looked up, stunned, as she recognized the voice of Mr. Bob Simpson, who perched on the corner of her desk, undeterred by her rudeness.

"Oh, Mr. Simpson, I'm so sorry," Susan said. "I was so caught up in this data—"

"Never mind," he said. His pale blue eyes crinkled as he gave his toothy smile. "I'll bet you're very busy. I wanted to personally welcome you to the Corporate Challenge team. And I've got some good news."

"You do? For me? I mean, does it have to do with me or, um . . ." Susan clammed up, angry with herself for being unprepared for just such an encounter. Here was her golden chance to press her wish list onto the president, and she was stammering and blushing.

"I was looking over your proposal on the waste emissions at the incinerator today. It's brilliant."

"Yes. Yes, it is," Susan said. She sat back with a jolt and waited for the usual shoot-down. Instead, Mr. Simpson stood up, grinning like Santa Claus.

"You've got the green light," he said. "Take any funds you need. I don't know how it slipped past me these last four months."

"Five months," Susan corrected. "And I won't let you down, Mr. Simpson. I'll work night and day."

"Please, call me Bob. And don't work too hard. We want our athletes well rested for the Corporate Challenge." He passed by Ingrid at the doorway to the office and gave her his best bucktooth smile.

"I got the proposal," Susan said to Ingrid, still shocked by the easy way the president had broken the news.

"Way to go, kid!" Ingrid crowed. "Finally the top brass sees how brilliant you are."

"But he thinks I'm an athlete," Susan said worriedly. "What if I let the team down on the Corporate Challenge weekend and he fires me?"

"Forget it," Ingrid said with a laugh. "They'd never replace you. And besides, you've been in training for over a week now. Are you still hurting every time you move, poor kid?"

"Not as much. Actually I'm almost enjoying the

training. And running feels so good once you stop.'' Susan cupped her chin in her hand, recalling the way Fear had teased her for wanting to lie down on the soft grass at the end of the three miles, insisting instead that they walk a bit to slow their heart rates. She'd let him lead her to the path and made him laugh when she'd dragged her feet like a prisoner on the way to the gallows. What a deep and happy laugh he had.

Susan felt a tap on her shoulder.

''Wind currents over the Antarctic,'' Ingrid said.

''Hmmm?''

Ingrid waved a hand in front of her friend's face. ''Hello in there. Lights on, nobody home. Susan, speak.''

''Sorry. You need some data, right?'' Susan said, slowly focusing on the business at hand. ''I'm not myself today.''

''Thinking about who I think you're thinking about?'' Ingrid asked with narrowed eyes. ''He is one good-looking man.''

''He's certainly gorgeous,'' Susan agreed, recalling the tangle of Fear's thick lashes, his shaggy black hair that went off in all directions.

''And he really likes you. Don't you think?'' Ingrid said.

''I can't tell. I don't really know Fear,'' Susan said dreamily.

''Fear? You're weird, Susan.''

''Not that kind of Fear. Fear Burns.''

"Yes, Fear burns and love hurts. I still don't know what you're talking about. *I'm* talking about Calvin Hart."

"Calvin Hart?" Susan said in astonishment.

"Susan!" Ingrid wailed. "What's come over you? Tell me. You can do it. Call on the scientist lurking beneath the airhead."

Turning, Susan checked the doorway glass for stray employees and lowered her voice to a whisper. "I took your advice. Personal trainer." She held a finger to her lips and jerked her head to the open door. "No one must know."

"A personal trainer. Terrific!" Ingrid yelped.

"Shhh!" Susan commanded. "The rest of the team thinks I'm a seasoned athlete. If word gets out that I can hardly walk a mile, let alone run three miles, I'm doomed. I will be banished from the Challenge. No Challenge, no weekend. No weekend, no schmoozing. No schmoozing, no promotion, no nothing."

"I won't tell," Ingrid promised. "But it's admirable that you are striving for fitness, even if your motive is completely misguided. You don't have to act like it's a crime."

"Trust me. It's better to keep this quiet."

Ingrid leaned back against the file cabinet, crossed her long, muscled legs, and ran a critical eye over Susan's compact form. "You look better already, Susan," she announced.

''Nonsense. I just started,'' Susan grumbled, secretly pleased by the compliment.

''But you do! Your complexion is blooming. Your hair is shiny. You glow with health. Your inner beauty is showing through.''

Susan eyed her friend with the pitying look she reserved for sick kittens and lost children. ''You, my dear, are a true fitness nut. Or just a nut. So tell me, Fitness Queen, what do I have in store for me with 'air?' Fear said I'd meet with 'air' tomorrow.''

''Air? Is that another trainer, maybe? Fear and Air, the dynamic duo. Very elemental.''

''No. It's something to do with the training. Fear was quite secretive.''

''Maybe he's going to take you skydiving.''

''Not in this lifetime,'' Susan scoffed.

''Okay. Perhaps he said 'hair,' as in put some hair on your chest,'' Ingrid teased.

''Definitely not! Besides, Fear has enough chest hair for both of us.''

''Hmm. So you noticed his chest hair.''

''I couldn't help it,'' Susan said. ''He wears a tank top and shorts, so I couldn't not notice.''

Ingrid snapped her fingers. ''I've got it,'' she said. ''He said 'err' as in 'to err is human.' ''

''I'll find out soon enough,'' Susan said. A small smile played on the corners of her mouth as she recalled the mischievous sparkle in Fear's eyes.

''Wait!'' Ingrid cried. ''I've figured it out. He's going to run you till you drop and then give you air. Mouth to mouth," she added, wiggling her eyebrows.

"Oh, Ingrid." Susan moaned. "I'm so afraid I'll never get in shape. Fear has confidence in me that I just don't have in myself."

"He's the expert. If Fear sees potential, then you shouldn't be discouraged."

"When I'm with him, I believe in myself. There's a calm determination in Fear that makes me feel really good. But as soon as I start to think logically, I worry that I'm pursuing a lost cause." Susan chewed her lip and gazed up at her friend.

"You really like him," Ingrid said incredulously. "I've never heard you talk so honestly about any man before."

Susan quickly shook her head. "No. I mean, I like him, but he's not my type. Of course, Fear is intriguing, but can you see me dating a jock who works in a gym?"

"Yes, I can," Ingrid said.

"Who asked you?" Susan snapped, annoyed by the sappy know-it-all look on her girlfriend's face.

"*You* asked me. And Fear Burns sounds like a perfectly wonderful human being who makes you feel good about yourself."

"He works in a gym. I'm a scientist. It doesn't bear discussing. So let me get these stats for you." Expertly, Susan called up the data and had the information emerge on the laser printer over in Ingrid's department, an innovation she herself had set in motion at Silent Controls. ''Done!'' she said smugly.

''Brilliant girl. Thanks. And I should let you know, Calvin is asking me all sorts of questions about you. I guess you've managed to catch his attention after all.''

''I'm no longer interested in Calvin.''

''What!'' Ingrid said, pretending to be shocked. ''But he is your type, exactly. Remember? An intellectual with burning ambition. Isn't that what you want? Or didn't the man meet all of your qualifications?''

Susan tilted back in her chair and put her hands on her head, all confidence and control. ''We didn't click.''

''So the scientist admits that some aspects of attraction are beyond the realm of analysis?''

Susan flipped her hair behind her ear and scowled. ''You make me sound so calculating,'' she said.

''You are far too logical. Loosen up and relax a bit. Have fun with this Fear Burns. You never know what might happen.''

''Thanks for the advice,'' Susan said. ''And on your way out, take these.''

With a flourish, Susan pulled the crystal dish of jujubes from the drawer and managed to pass one last handful over to her friend.

* * *

On Saturday morning, Fear and Susan sat at his usual table at Flap Jack's Pancake House, a table for two right beside the plate glass window that looked out over the fenced-in patio. Eire, an enormous furry wolfhound, lay contentedly dozing in the hot sunshine, looking like an old shaggy rug left outside for far too long

"I should have guessed your mysterious 'air' was a pet dog," Susan said. "You look like a dog man to me. The outdoorsy type, I mean." Her cheeks were flushed from the run through the park, and the baby blue warm-up suit brought out the turquoise hues of her eyes. Even at this early hour, Susan wore her bright lipstick, and the coffee cup in front of her held a scarlet ring on the rim.

"A dog man," Fear said. "I've been called many things before, but never that."

Susan smiled. "I sure wanted to call you worse things than that after the first mile. I truly thought my legs were going to collapse under me, and my lungs hurt as if they were going to burst. But I did it! I finished the three miles and lived to tell the tale."

Fear covered her hand with his own, briefly, too quickly, and released it. His long fingers fiddled with his coffee cup, as if he were embarrassed by the contact. "Aren't you glad I pushed you now?" he asked.

Susan nodded, touched by the sincerity in Fear's expression. Gone was the cocky pirate's smile, the belligerent coaxing that had driven her to push her body to the limit during the run. Instead he seemed truly pleased with her performance.

"Eire seems to bring out the best in people," Fear said, with an affectionate glance outside at the sleeping animal. "A dog runs so easily, so delighted by the run itself, and that enthusiasm seems to rub off on whoever is with him."

"Eire is a great dog. I never had a dog when I grew up, so I never really liked them. But Eire is so sensitive. He seemed to slow down when I most needed it. But I did it. Three miles!" Susan marveled.

"Stick with me, Silver Sue, and you'll achieve every goal you've ever set. Every physical goal, that is."

Susan caught the edge in his voice and looked over to meet his eyes. The fierce scrutiny she saw there unnerved her, and she swiveled around to scan the crowded restaurant for a waitress. "I would say that I deserve the tall stack of chocolate-chip pancakes now, don't I? And I'm ravenous. I can smell the chocolate from here."

At that moment the disheveled waitress set two plates down, each laden with steamy pancakes topped with a slab of melting butter. Susan's first bite melted in her mouth and she savored the unique flavor combination.

"Good?" Fear asked, dowsing his blueberry pancakes with a torrent of vanilla syrup.

"Excellent," Susan replied. "But these pancakes

aren't the chocolate chip I ordered.'' She took another bite and chewed slowly, her head thoughtfully tilted to one side. ''I taste apricot and something else. A delicious aftertaste.''

Fear took her hand and guided a forkful to his own mouth. His eyes lit up as he tasted the flavorful concoction.

''Cashews,'' he announced. ''Apricots and cashews. Delicious, but definitely not chocolate. Do you want to send your order back to the kitchen and get chocolate chip?''

Susan shook her head so her hair danced merrily. ''No way. I've stumbled across a new favorite. What an odd combination, but it works somehow, doesn't it, Fear?''

''Yes,'' Fear answered, his dark eyes narrowed. ''Often it's the odd combinations that work best. Even with people.''

''Yes. Opposites attract, right? You see friends and lovers with outwardly nothing in common, yet they make the happiest couples.''

Susan drew a sharp breath. Was he talking about the two of them? Certainly they made an odd combination, he so focused on the physical parts of life while she passed most of her days using only her brains. And yet they did make a good couple. They both shared an offbeat sense of humor, they each had a streak of perfectionism that drove them, although in totally different pursuits. And when Fear was beside her, Susan liked the way her head came up to his jaw-line, so she only had to tilt her face a bit to see his face. And they both loved to eat, Susan thought, as she watched Fear dig into the huge breakfast. She smiled at Fear and spun the trolley on the side of the table, laden with tiny silver jugs, looking for the chocolate sauce.

"I might as well add a little twist to this combination," she said ruefully. "And I was looking forward to the chocolate sauce. Here, please take one of my pancakes. Delicious as they are, I don't think even I can finish the enormous amount of food on this plate."

"Apricots and cashews," Fear said, and shook his head in wonder. "Isn't it funny how when you don't get what you want, often the thing you end up with turns out to be better?"

Susan regarded him sharply. Was he making a point again? About them, or about life in general? If only she knew him well enough to know the answer.

"Are you referring to my desire to run Silent Controls? Because you are wrong. I would not be happy to get the consolation prize. I want to be president, and I can't imagine anything better."

Fear's face fell into serious lines and he set down his knife and fork and took a long drink of coffee, his eyes moodily turned out the window. "I wasn't talking about you at all," he said finally. "I was thinking of my own life, and how it's changed from what I originally wanted. Or thought I wanted."

Susan had to restrain herself from following her instinct to reach out and stroke the worry from his brow. For all his heavy muscles and deep masculine voice, Fear seemed at this moment like a little boy lost in a bad daydream.

"What did you want, Fear, that you couldn't have?" Susan asked gently.

When he turned back to face her, Susan's breath caught in her throat. Those dark eyes were black with emotion, and gave off a light like liquid shadows full of secrets that lay just below the surface, and for a moment she was absolutely sure he was going to reveal a terrible secret. Instead, after a few seconds of struggle, Fear grinned broadly, a carefree pirate once again.

"What I want is that last apricot-and-cashew pancake," he joked.

"Consider it yours," she said lightly, relieved yet disappointed that the moment had passed.

On the way home, Fear took her through the shortcut in the park that she never knew existed. The scent of new grass and open lilac blossoms mingled headily with the babble of the brook beside the path. Eire loped ahead ecstatically, chasing squirrels back up the path and into the leaning willows. Everywhere on the spreading lawns, people enjoyed the fine Saturday morning. As she watched the couples strolling hand in hand, it occurred to Susan that she and Fear must appear like lovers out together for an early walk. Shyly, she glanced up at him and smiled.

"I feel good," she admitted. "And I like being outside. It makes me feel so awake. Like every sense is alive."

Fear nodded sagely. "It's a proven fact that an office building is the worst place to spend time if you want to stay healthy."

Susan frowned and quickened her pace across the log bridge that spanned the river. "That's true. However, it's my job to improve air quality inside these buildings, and statistics prove that interior environments are steadily improving, thanks to scientists like me."

"I still can't comprehend why a young and beautiful woman like you wants to run a huge company."

"No, I don't expect you to understand," Susan said huffily.

"I won't understand because I'm just a dumb jock?" Fear said. He pulled up short underneath a spreading maple and crossed his arms over his broad chest.

"I didn't say that," Susan muttered, flustered by his abrupt anger.

"But that's what you mean, isn't it?" he persisted. "You think you're so superior because you're a trained scientist and you have a high-status job, but you can't understand that there are people who don't give a hoot about position and wealth."

"Maybe it's not about position and wealth," Susan said, truly angry now. "Maybe I get satisfaction from using my brains to truly change the world, even if I can only do it one step at a time, one building at a time. At least when I go to sleep at night, I know that I have done my part to save the environment."

"And you have to be president of the whole corporation to save the environment?" Fear said. He bent down to grab Eire, who had appeared to protest the unplanned stop, and clipped a leash on the collar.

"No," Susan said, falling into step with Fear across the lawn. "I have to be president to do it my way. Is it a crime to want to make something of my life?"

Fear gestured across the field, where a woman in a white dress sat with two small golden-haired children, all three of them laughing while the gentle breeze ruffled their clothes.

"Look at that mother," Fear said. "Do you think she feels her life is wasted?"

Susan shook her head. "Not if that's what she wants to do with her life," she stated truthfully.

"That is the most important part of a woman's life," Fear said emphatically. "A mother's love for her children. If love makes the world go round, it's the maternal love that sets it spinning. And there are too many unhappy children being raised by nannies."

Susan's retort was lost as Eire broke free and made a beeline toward the dancing children, proceeding to knock over the toddler and spread dirty pawprints along the woman's dress before Fear managed to gain control of the leash. Susan arrived at the gathering in time to hear Fear's apology.

"You have very brave children. Big dogs like Eire can be intimidating sometimes."

"Oh, they're not my children," the woman said. "I'm the nanny and their mother had to work today, so I'm stuck on a weekend. But I don't mind, really, on such a beautiful day."

As they walked out of the park and onto the city streets, neither of them spoke. Susan resisted the urge to mock Fear and his sentimental and rather old-fashioned view of motherhood. She sensed that the issue ran deep for him, out of some part of his past that had left him hurt, and when they reached the apartment door, she was the first to speak.

"I really enjoyed the morning," Susan said. "And thanks a lot for breakfast."

Fear shoved his hands into his track pants pockets and looked up at the sky. "I had a good time too. We'll do it again."

"Okay. I'd like that."

"Actually, my house is just around the corner and down two streets. We're practically neighbors. I'll have to pop by someday and borrow a cup of sugar. With your sweet tooth, you'll have sugar in your cupboards."

"You have your own house?" Susan said. No single person she knew owned a house. Although she could well afford a house, it never occurred to her to buy one, although the idea, now that it came up, appealed to her.

"A bungalow. I could never live in an apartment. I'd feel trapped," Fear said, his eyes fixed on the peak of her bowed lips. Nervously, he ran a hand through his hair and encountered the newly cropped head.

"Well, I guess you disapprove of almost every facet of my life," Susan said. "My workplace, my professional ambitions, and now my choice of home. It's a wonder that you can abide spending any time with me at all."

Fear's look of surprise changed to delight as he looked down into her haughty little face. He pulled her to him and pressed her head into his chest in more of a headlock than a hug.

"Oh, you're not so bad, Silver Sue. I'm just going to have to educate you."

"That's a laugh," Sue said into his shirt. "I'm probably the most educated person you know."

"I doubt that," he said, releasing her. She blinked up and tried to smooth her rumpled hair. "See you Monday."

Then he was gone, with Eire trotting beside him down the street, leaving behind the sensation of his strong embrace and the memory of the warm scent of his chest.

Susan let herself into her apartment and saw first the stack of textbooks on the dining-room table. Instead of stimulating her into action, the books made her feel more tired than ever. After the fresh air and sunshine, the apartment seemed dark and close, and she threw open all the windows and took off her shoes and socks. The enormity of her busy life hit her like a ton of bricks and for the first time in her life Susan wondered if she could cope with the goals she had set. She was overwhelmed by the training sessions ahead, the pages of notes she had to study for the night school courses, and the new assignment at work that was bound to mean late nights and overtime. How simply the morning had passed with Fear by her side, outside and running around with the freedom and exhilaration of childhood. Susan had forgotten what having fun was like. Not the fun of a monumental entertainment, not a planned and catered cocktail party, just plain, messing-about fun. She realized that merely being with Fear made her feel safe and happy, until he started in about her lifestyle, of course. What she didn't need was anyone to pass judgment on the way she lived. And another thing she truly didn't need was this unshakable, all-consuming desire to take Fear Burns in her arms and never let him go.

Chapter Five

Susan eyed the pile of papers on her desk and wondered how she had survived the past week with no more lasting damage than some sore muscles and two dark circles under her normally bright eyes. Finally, the report for the president was wrapped up and on his desk and Susan could now concentrate on her usual business. She had sailed through the exam last night at the night school course and the next session was not due to start until summer's end, so she had a bit of breathing room. If it weren't for Fear Burns and his rigid training schedule, Susan's life would be much like it always was—staid, quiet, and filled with books and junk food.

Susan swallowed as she looked over at the steaming tray of onion rings on Nelson's desk. *It isn't fair,* she thought. *I've worked so hard; I deserve a treat.* Except that if she slipped up on her diet, she would have to tell Fear at the volleyball practice tonight. Lately he'd questioned her about every facet of her life, from the duration of her night's sleep to her scheduled meal plans. It seemed as if she spoke to him or saw him every day, and it got no easier to resist his charms. When she was with him, she admired his warm humor and his quiet strength and forgot all about how unsuitable he would be as a boyfriend. All Fear had to do was smile and ask her to go that extra mile or hoist that heavier weight, and she was putty in his hands. Only after she'd cooled down and got back to her office did she find herself rationalizing away her attraction to him. Even then, Susan found herself actively looking forward to the time she spent with Fear, and it didn't seem to matter to her whether that time involved running with Eire and his master through the woodland paths that lined the city or several exhausting hours at Get Fit with Fear at her side cajoling her through a workout. Even the volleyball was enjoyable. The corporate team welcomed Fear's expertise into their ranks and Susan did nothing to correct their mistaken impression that Fear Burns was anything more than a boyfriend out for an evening's fun. Susan laughed softly as she recalled how easily Fear had slipped into the boyfriend role at the last volleyball practice, even taking her hand as they left the high-school gym together and gazing deeply into her eyes.

Strange how good it felt when he slid his arm across her shoulders and she nestled perfectly into the space beneath, almost as if they truly were meant to be together. But that was part of the act, Susan reminded herself firmly.

With one last longing glance at Nelson's onion rings, Susan opened her own paper bag and scowled at the grainy bread and vegetable sticks. She was so bored with healthy eating. Visions of pizza and doughnuts and big juicy cheeseburgers danced in her head. Surely if she slid off the health food wagon for one day no one would be any the wiser. After a moment's hesitation, when her conscience struggled for the upper hand, Susan stood up and dropped the lunch bag into the garbage can with a resounding thud.

"I'm going out," she announced. "And don't ask me where," she warned in response to Nelson's know-it-all smile.

The weather had turned from great to perfect and the only clouds in the blue sky drifted by as white and puffy as a child's drawing. Everywhere in the streets and parkettes people strolled by, delighted by the early summer sunshine. In the greenbelt area tucked behind the office buildings, Susan found exactly what she was looking for—the dear, familiar hot dog vendor with a cart full of candy and potato chips.

Feeling very pleased with herself, she found an empty park bench beside the shady footpath and opened the carry-out box, not feeling the least bit guilty about the sugary pop, the big bag of ketchup chips, or the hot dog smothered in chili sauce and onions. *I deserve this,* Susan thought, as she leaned back and raised her face to the sunshine, determined to savor each mouthful of the forbidden food. If only Fear was not so proud of her progress and what he called her will of steel, she would not feel such a rush of guilt as she broke her promise to him. And Susan did not doubt that somehow Fear would manage to extract a confession from her tonight at the volleyball practice when he pinned her with those piercing black eyes and asked her how her day had been. He had an unnerving honesty about him that made her weigh the answers to even his most casual questions, to think before she spoke, and yet Susan couldn't shake the suspicion that Fear Burns was not entirely as he seemed. The more time she spent with him the more she glimpsed the hidden undercurrents of a darker side to the devil-may-care athlete who cared only for sports and good times.

Susan took a long sip of pop from the straw and recalled the hint of sadness in Fear's soulful gaze as he spoke of Ireland. Perhaps the melancholy air was merely homesickness for his boyhood country, but Susan sensed an anger there as well, and every instinct told her that a profound hurt had driven Fear from everything he knew to come over to Canada and start a new life. In spite of his all-consuming love of sports, Fear had a sensitive streak that showed up in the gentle way he allayed her fears about her athletic abilities, his sympathetic ear as she relayed the trauma of her father's early death. He knew exactly when to tone down his drill-sergeant manners and when to counter her own weakness with sharp commands.

Fear was no dumb jock, she was beginning to understand that now. His mind was sharp, and in any discussion she'd had with him, his depth of knowledge enhanced the conversation. And he seemed truly interested in her meteorological research, and grasped even the most scientific details. It was a puzzle, then, why a man with Fear's obvious intelligence and curiosity would choose to spend his life in a career devoted to the body.

Susan sighed, picked up the box of candy, and stared at it miserably. Already she felt as if she'd let Fear down. And who was she cheating really? Herself and herself alone.

"Are you going to eat that or just stare at it?" a voice said. Susan closed her eyes and wished the words away, hoping it was her guilt that had dredged up Fear's deep lilting voice. But when she opened them again, there he was in his white shorts, his tank top damp with sweat. The woman beside him was shaped like an Olympic athlete. She was taller than Fear by a bit and her blond ponytail on top of her head further elongated her.

"Oh, hello, Fear," Susan said in a small voice. She stood up more to block from his sight the carry-out carton on the bench, and put the candy behind her back.

Fear put his hands on his waist. "Too late, Silver Sue," he said. "I saw the stash. I'm surprised you of all people can't follow the rules for a few short weeks."

Instantly, Susan's back went up. It wasn't fair— she'd been so good about this tiresome training session, and Fear had no idea the extent of her junk food addiction. "And I'm surprised you're spying on your clients," Susan snapped. "You know perfectly well I work on this block, and you deliberately came this way at lunch to see if you could catch me in the act."

Fear laughed down at her angry little face. "You flatter yourself. Katrina and I are on a ten-mile run, so we'll be covering a lot of ground. It's a coincidence that I've caught you red-handed."

Impatiently, Katrina started jogging on the spot so her ponytail wiggled from side to side.

"I would have told you," Susan muttered. "I know you won't believe me, but this is the first time I had a lapse."

Fear took a step toward her. "What makes you think I won't believe you?" he asked softly. Susan looked up into his face, all too aware that in her high heels she stood taller against him than usual and their lips could easily come together with very little effort. Without thinking, she leaned ever so slightly toward him and tilted her chin up. How wonderful it would be to stop talking, to stop all thoughts, to lean just a little closer and feel his mouth on hers.

"Fear!" Katrina called. "We must run!"

Fear jumped back as if shocked by a blast of reality. "I've got to go."

"Of course. Don't let me interfere in your personal life."

"Katrina is a client."

"She is?" Susan said, annoyed by the wave of relief this information brought.

"Yes. She wants to run a marathon."

Fear and Susan shared a secret smile that seemed to irritate the waiting woman. "Fear! Please say goodbye to your girlfriend now. I must run!" Katrina said.

"Until tonight," Fear said. Quickly he took her hand, dropped it, and followed an indignant Katrina away down the footpath. Humming happily, Susan finished the hot dog and pitched the potato chips into a nearby trash can.

The volleyball practice had gone well and Susan should have felt proud of herself, yet she couldn't shake her melancholy mood as she sat on the edge of the bleachers and waited for Fear to emerge from the locker room. The high school gym where the practice had taken place brought unpleasant memories for Susan of the humiliation of always being the last girl chosen for any team game. She had simply been too short to excel at basketball or volleyball, too delicate to survive the assaults of field hockey players, and all too uncoordinated to stay on a balance beam, even though her body was slim and compact. And Susan had so wanted to be a part of the sports culture at school that she joined the cheerleading squad just to get involved with after-school games. Her reputation as a bookworm had not diminished, however. Even boys with a scholarly bent had resented her superior marks.

No, Susan thought, high school had not been the best years of her life. The best years were yet to come, she thought, her heart quickening as she saw Fear cross the shiny floor, his stride sure and steady, his crisp hair still damp from the shower.

Fear held open the heavy exit door and Susan brushed by him into the windy night. The warm air pushed against her, fresh and charged with the hint of rain that promised changes ahead.

"I never thought I'd be able to say this, but I was good tonight," Susan said, with a little dance of joy when her feet hit the dewy grass.

Fear grinned down at her and she felt the space between them spark with a strange energy that drew him closer, although his feet had not moved an inch.

"Truly, Silver Sue. Truly you were marvelous."

"Better than marvelous. I actually scored a few points," Susan said.

"All thanks to your extraordinarily brilliant trainer."

Without warning, Fear trapped her head in the crook of his elbow and pressed his face against her hair. A powerful jolt hit her as she inhaled the sharply scented skin of his forearm and felt the curly hair tickle her lips. Frightened by her own reaction, Susan broke free and stood facing him on the sidewalk under a street-light, where she could see his face clearly. Fear's expression was carefully neutral as he waited for her to speak.

"Yes. It's true, Fear. I have the best coach in the world. I couldn't do any of this without you. Physically or mentally." Impulsively, Susan stood on tiptoe and planted a rosy kiss on his cheek. Feeling the rough whiskers against her skin, her hands on the hard swell of his shoulders, Susan was acutely aware that he was a very attractive man.

As she backed away, Fear's strong fingers encircled her biceps and lifted her up almost off the ground, and suddenly his mouth was on hers, not so gentle now, but with a firm pressure almost too much to bear. Yet Fear didn't linger. He eased her back down to the pavement and Susan stood dazed in the ring of lamp-light. She gaped up at him, stunned by his boldness, amazed by the power in his kiss. Yet Fear seemed unmoved by the same powerful forces of doubt and longing sweeping in a wave through her. As if nothing momentous had passed, Fear grinned his pirate's smile and shoved his hands into the pockets of his shorts.

"So I'd say you have nothing to worry about at the

Corporate Challenge weekend,'' Fear said easily, and resumed the stroll as if that earth-shattering moment was only a dream.

Susan scrambled after him and fell into his stride. After a long silence, while the commotion in her head made it impossible to focus on any one thought, she cleared her throat. ''You don't have to walk me home.''

''I thought *you* were walking *me* home,'' Fear said. ''Anyway, here's your apartment.''

Suddenly chilled in spite of the warm breeze, Susan zipped her jacket as they stopped in front of the brightly lit lobby. At this point, it seemed only natural for Susan to invite Fear up to her place for a cold drink, yet she hesitated. If that first kiss was any indication of the power this man had over her, Susan was not about to risk the consequences of where a casual drink might lead her heart.

''So I guess this is good night then,'' she said. Fear's face was half in shadow and his dark eyes stood out vividly.

''Aren't you going to ask me up?'' he asked.

''No!'' Susan said. ''I'm tired. And I don't think it would be a good idea.'' Her knees weakened as his finger traced a curve down her cheekbone to her lip.

''Why are you so nervous, Silver Sue?'' Fear asked softly.

''Nervous? Me? That's ridiculous! Why on earth

would I be nervous?'' Susan forced a laugh that came out as a breathy gasp.

''Susan, you're as high-strung as a racehorse,'' Fear said. His hands found her shoulders and he massaged them with his thumbs in a soothing, repetitive stroke. ''I would never hurt you,'' he said, inching closer. ''You know that, don't you? And I'd never make you do anything you don't want to do.''

Susan stiffened. ''Fear, every time I see you, you make me do things I don't want to do,'' she said.

''Your muscles are tight,'' Fear murmured as his fingers traced the nape of her neck. At the end of their exploration his hands reached underneath her shiny hair and cupped her head, tilting her face up to his.

''You're so beautiful,'' he whispered. His hands held her face steady as he bent to kiss her. This time, it was Fear who lingered. Susan's nerves jangled and her body felt stiff. Her instincts demanded that she turn and flee, yet his arms felt so right around her. Besides, she had no room to maneuver between his body and the brick wall behind her.

Abruptly, he backed away, sliding his hands down over her sides, leaving a trail of fire where his fingers had touched. ''Let's go up and see your place,'' Fear said, serious now. His eyes were black as windows in a midnight sky, full of hope and trust.

''Fear!'' she cried. Unable to meet his eyes, aware that she exuded the same raw emotion, she dropped her face against his chest and burrowed like a frightened child.

Instantly, his arms circled her protectively now and he crooned soft words into her ear. ''It's okay, Susan. Never mind. Some other time.''

She shook her head against his chest, refusing to look up until she could straighten her thoughts. There would be no ''other time.''

''Susan,'' Fear said. He placed his hand under her chin and lifted her face up. Silently, Susan studied his handsome face and saw in his expression great tenderness and humor and again that disturbing sadness that she did not want to add to. But he was smiling now, as if he didn't want to make her feel bad.

''The forecast is for rain tomorrow, so we'll need a bright and early start. I'll meet you right here on your doorstep at seven-thirty.''

''How about eight? I'll need coffee for wake-up fuel.''

''Compromise. Seven-forty-five. And if you're a no-show I'm coming up to drag you out of bed.''

Susan startled at the image. ''I'll be right here in this lobby,'' she said. ''You don't have to drag me out of bed.''

''Sweet dreams, Silver Sue,'' Fear said, and started down the steps as she unlocked the outer door.

Susan kept the door open and watched him walk away. His legs were darkly tanned against the white of his shorts.

"Hey, Fear!"

He turned back, shadows deep beneath his cheek-bones, his hair tossed by the night wind. All at once, he seemed so strong and confident, so savvy in the ways of the world, that Susan was glad she hadn't invited him upstairs. Even now, she thought resentfully, he was probably expecting her to change her mind, like every other woman he had dealings with.

"I forgot to ask," Susan said, her chin lifted proudly. "What are we doing at seven-forty-five?"

"Running, me darling," Fear replied with an exaggerated lilt. "You're good, but we still have to whip you into shape. Only one more weekend till the Challenge. You're not out of the woods yet, Silver Sue."

Not out of the woods, indeed, Susan thought as she let herself into her apartment. It was Fear himself leading her into the woods, with his confusing messages and devastating good looks. That aura of sadness was most likely an act to gain sympathy with reluctant females, and yes, the ploy had affected her, for all her intelligence. Thank goodness she had the brains to realize that the siren call of her emotions had nothing to do with a rational choice of mate. Life must progress with some adherence to plan, and right now she had to concern herself with the competition for the vice presidency. *With Fear Burns throwing a monkey wrench into my well-laid plans,* she thought, as she belted her terry robe over her waist, *I'll be lucky to get through the next week without losing my mind entirely.*

And the Corporate Challenge weekend was a great place to meet eligible businessmen, men who were equally ambitious and involved in more intellectual pursuits than Fear Burns, and luckily Fear would not be at the wilderness lodge with his tyrannical commands. It would be a weekend where she could further her career goals, make important business contacts, and carry on with her life. No Fear Burns at her side.

Susan turned on the hot water in the tub and watched the water run, puzzled by the deadweight in the pit of her stomach whenever she imagined the Challenge weekend. Was it simply a bad case of nerves? Or was the idea of competing without Fear beside her too hard to deal with? After dumping in an excessive amount of bath oil, Susan absently added half a jar of bubble bath and slowly sat on the edge of the tub.

It's not as if I'll be all alone at the wilderness lodge, she consoled herself. *Ingrid will be there, and she's the best friend anyone could imagine. And Calvin will be very attentive, that's for sure. And the president and his wife will be there. Buzz and Natalie seem like a nice couple. It will be fun,* she thought firmly, as she lowered herself into the steamy bubbles.

But try as she might, she could not banish the image of Fear and his sad dark eyes. In no way had he intimated that he would like to accompany her on the weekend away. In fact, he had gone out of his way to assure her that she would put on a magnificent performance at the three-mile race and quite capably handle herself at the volleyball tournament. Whenever Susan had worried aloud about her abilities, Fear refused to listen. He had steadily built her confidence until there was no reason to feel she couldn't go the course alone, independent of the man who had brought her to this level of competence. So why did she feel so completely devastated at the thought of competing without Fear Burns there to cheer her on?

Susan frowned at the ceiling and popped a bubble with her toe. Logically, there was no question that she was capable of running without a coach. It made perfect sense that this last week of training would suffice, that she would no longer need the services of a personal trainer. Sure, her body was in fine form, better than it had ever been, but emotionally, Susan decided, she was a wreck. Fear had managed to mess her up so badly that she couldn't face the weekend without him. What would he say if she invited him to come away to the wilderness lodge with her?

Susan sat up and sloshed the bath bubbles over the side, excited by the idea of a weekend with Fear. As her coach, he had a legitimate reason to be there. Her teammates would assume she was bringing her boyfriend, except for Ingrid, who knew the truth, and who would be delighted that Susan had relented on the matter of Fear Burns. Not that she had really relented.

Surely it was only because of his steadying influence that Susan needed Fear beside her. So many questions, Susan thought, as she got out of the tub and wrapped herself in a towel.

I'll wait, Susan decided, *until Fear himself brings up the subject of the Challenge weekend.* By then she'd have sorted out the bewildering ambiguities of her emotions and worked out the best possible solution. In the past her mind had always rescued her from her from sabotaging her own plans with messy emotions. Never before had her superior intellect failed to come up with the best plan, and she was confident that all would turn out well.

At the end of the week, Fear leaned moodily against the back wall of the fitness room and looked out over the crowded machines where men and women worked out to the throbbing beat of rock music. Get Fit attracted a young and energetic crowd, and bursts of conversation and merry laughter combined with the music and the clang of barbells and raised the noise level to a point were Fear wanted to pack it all in and go out for a solitary run in the summer twilight. Usually the sight of people enjoying the health club he'd created from his own bare-bones dreams gave Fear a sense of pride in his accomplishment, but this evening all he wanted to do was find a quiet spot to sort out the tangle of his emotions. All this last week of his personal training contract for Susan Silver, he had felt an ominous shadow hanging over his head and he'd been unable to distinguish if his uneasiness stemmed from the fact that Susan would no longer be in his life after this time together, or if his subconscious mind had registered something he'd been unwilling to admit to himself—that he was inextricably in love with a woman who showed all the signs of being a woman who put career first and all other aspects of life a distant second. Susan puzzled him. Her self-confidence was strong, but he saw huge holes of insecurity that made him want to protect her. The man in him demanded that he be her knight in shining armor, yet here was no damsel in distress. Far from helpless, Susan was intelligent and independent, so full of life and ready to see the humor in any situation. When he was with her, Fear didn't allow himself to imagine a future together, until now, that is, he thought, scowling at a pert brunette who flounced by with a flirtatious smile.

Now that their time together was over, now that there would be no legitimate reason to stay in contact, Fear found himself wondering how he could cope with a future bereft of Susan's company. And if he allowed himself to follow his heart, to be with Susan forever, how could he steel himself for the very real possibility that the future would repeat the past and his disastrous marriage to the social-climbing Mary who had betrayed him? Although, as it turned out, his departure from Ireland and the vainglorious medical career had turned out to be a gift in disguise. *Whatever happens next,* he thought, *I'll still have fulfilled my dream of running my own club and having each day to spend as I like.* But now that thought alone refused to console him.

Madeline appeared at his side with a stack of phone messages. ''Are you ever going to return any of these?'' she asked, her pug nose wrinkled in exasperation. ''I don't know what's wrong with you today. All you do is mope about. Don't bother,'' she added, as Fear begin to rifle through the stack. ''There's nothing from Susan.''

''What makes you think I was checking for her calls?'' Fear asked, obviously irritated that his secretary had caught him out.

Madeline tapped her forefinger against her lip and weighed her response. Pity won out over disapproval. ''Fear, ask her out on a proper date. I know she'd jump at the chance. Susan Silver is crazy about you, no matter how cool she acts. I can tell these things.''

Fear narrowed his eyes so his long lashes cast a shadow on his cheeks. A harsh line stood out in his jaw as his teeth clenched. ''How many times have I told you that I would never allow myself to get involved with another career woman?''

''Yes, you've said that before, but—''

''Do you think I don't have a brain in my head? I learn from my past mistakes, and I'm happier right now than I've ever been in my entire adult life.''

Madeline pressed her lips together and grunted. "You don't look very happy at this particular moment. You have frown lines as deep as caves."

"I am very happy," Fear barked.

"Yes, you are, especially in the past few weeks, and do I have to remind you that the timing coincides with the moment Susan Silver walked through those double-glass doors and into your life? Fear, I don't want to interfere with your hard-set rules, but I can see that Susan is a good person, and she is as smitten with you as you are with her. I see the two of you in here with your heads together, shutting out the rest of the world. Fear, please don't be so stubborn."

"I'm not being stubborn, Madeline," Fear said sadly. "I'm being practical. We're not meant to be together. We're total opposites, and you know how much I detest the business world and everyone who buys into that lifestyle. And Susan Silver is going to go far at Silent Controls, you mark my words. Her mind is so extraordinary and so quick, and so convoluted, but brilliant."

In spite of his bad mood, Fear managed a faraway smile as he thought of Susan's childlike enthusiasm when she spoke about her job.

Madeline tapped his shoulder to get his attention. "I want to ask you a favor," she said, amused by his blatant relief that she had dropped the subject of Susan Silver.

"Anything, me darling," he said, once again in good humor.

"Can I get off work a little early tonight?" Madeline asked shyly.

"Hot date?" Fear teased, as he did every weekend, sure that Madeline had no such prospects in her dull life.

"As a matter of fact, yes, I do have a hot date," Madeline said haughtily. Fear all at once noticed her curled hair, the uncharacteristic eye makeup and short skirt, the aura of excitement that hung over his usually calm secretary.

"Of course, Madeline," he said, "leave anytime you like. I can close up here."

Madeline flushed under his perusal. "Would now be all right? I'll understand if you say no," she said.

Fear followed her quick glance to the exit doors and saw the younger man who'd been pursuing Madeline for months, gym bag in hand, freshly showered and eagerly waiting for his date.

"That young man wore you down, did he?" Fear laughed. "Whatever happened to your vow to never go near a younger member of the opposite sex?"

"I changed my mind," Madeline said simply.

A long pause ensued. Fear knew all too well what Madeline was implying—that rules changed and avenues once closed could open up. Madeline was trying to get him to see the benefits of flexibility. More than once she'd drawn his attention to the flaw in him that held him to a decision that would once have been legitimate but had needed to be reshaped. And always, she was right.

"Have a great time, Madeline," Fear said.

"Oh, I will," Madeline said.

"And don't do anything I wouldn't do," he joked.

"That will be hard," Madeline said over her shoulder, "since you don't appear to do anything."

Stung by her flippant criticism, Fear made his way to the office and sat down with his hand on the phone. He could do two things. He could start with the top message in the stack and return the phone calls, or he could phone Susan and insist that she allow him to go away with her for the weekend.

For a long time, Fear did neither. Then with his jaw set angrily, he picked up the stack of message sheets and punched in the top number.

Chapter Six

On Friday evening, Fear looked perfectly calm as he hoisted weights at Get Fit, but he was in a state of agitation unlike any he had ever experienced with any woman. One minute he wanted to phone Susan and demand that she take him with her to the weekend Challenge. Then, his rational mind jumped in to insist he let her go on with the rest of her life without him, that their relationship was never meant to be, that he'd be better off without her. Yet every time he thought of a future without Susan's sweet companionship, her quirky sense of fun, her warm and loving embrace, he felt a great despair sweep over him. Nothing had ever bothered him as much as the idea of his little Susan all alone at River Gorge Lodge pushing her delicate body through the hazards of a rugged terrain.

And harder to admit to himself was the power of the disturbing image of Susan in a slinky dress, her red lips in a saucy smile, surrounded by admiring men in suits, men who could dazzle her with their business acumen and smooth talk. In his heart, Fear sensed that Susan was beginning to feel as strongly about him as he felt about her, but she hadn't relented and asked him to go with her this weekend. And why not? Because their love was not meant to be, he decided grimly. Fear dropped the heavy barbell he was pumping and sat on the edge of the bench, analyzing his reflection in the full-length mirror in front of him. He saw a dark, powerfully built man, no longer with the open expression of youth, a man with a past that had set his features to a hard line.

Fear was not about to let the despair take over as it had so many years ago when his marriage and his life as a doctor had crumbled to dust. Never again was he going to let himself sink so low. He was going to rescue himself as he had saved himself from his own bad choices way back then, by throwing himself into his work.

Fear draped a towel over his neck, walked into Madeline's cubbyhole office, and stopped dead at the sight of a very familiar young man sprawled across the desk chatting happily with a seated Madeline. At Fear's entrance, the man slid off his perch away from Madeline and slipped from the room with only a brief nod in Fear's direction.

"What's wrong with lover boy?" Fear said, curious at the guilty way Madeline busied herself with the file in front of her. "Has he finally gotten it into that thick head of his that you're not interested in entertaining a younger man, no matter how persistent?"

Much to his amusement, Madeline's blush deepened and she sat up very straight. All pretense of work stopped and she crossed her arms over her chest.

"For your information, Eric and I hit it off and we're going out to the Jazz Café tonight."

"Good for you, Madeline," Fear said. "You've been working too hard lately and you deserve a good time."

"I hope I can find a baby-sitter on such short notice," Madeline said with a small worried frown. "I agreed to go out on this date without thinking. I really like Eric and he was so brave to keep asking me out when I gave him no encouragement at all. And I'm so glad he was persistent."

Fear saw a new sparkle transform Madeline's features into radiance. She exuded happiness and her smile was like a balm to his jangled nerves.

"Listen, Maddy, if you can't get your regular sitter I'd even cancel my pub night with my mates and mind the child."

"I know you would, Fear," Madeline said, failing to hide the emotion in her voice. "And I have you to thank for making me see the error of my ways. Why on earth should I deprive myself of Eric's company merely because of the gap in our ages?''

''Exactly what I've been telling you since the poor guy started mooning around you,'' Fear said, flopping into the armchair across from the desk and resting his hands on his head.

Madeline eyed him shrewdly. ''So you agree that preconceived notions about who is worthy of our attention should be put to the test now and then?''

Fear dropped his hands down to his lap. ''I guess so,'' he replied warily as he noticed the glint in his secretary's eyes.

''So why aren't you admitting to yourself that you're head over heels in love with a career woman?'' Madeline said with her hands spread out in front her, pleading with him to understand. ''Despite every vow you've ever made about getting involved with a working woman, you have found a lady who makes you feel good, a lady who is so right for you, and you're pulling back. I can see it happening when the two of you are together here.''

Fear's large hands began to fidget in his lap and he drew his thick brows together as if he could glare hard enough to silence the earnest woman in front of him. There were truths he didn't want to confront. Certainly he hadn't been quite himself since Silver Sue walked into his health club, but the strange sensations in the pit of his stomach, the light-headedness he felt whenever he accidentally brushed against her—surely that was only the reaction of any male to such a powerfully attractive woman. His response to her as a woman was intense and immediate, but that was only natural, since she was arrestingly beautiful, with a subtly curved and graceful body. And she smelled so sweet, like vanilla cookies. Fear smiled as he recalled how wide her eyes could grow when she succumbed to an attack of nerves. Susan was so childlike in her honesty, so brave in the face of vulnerability, that all his notions of what made a successful career woman had been shattered as he got to know her.

Instead of the callous aggression he'd seen in his ex-wife as she clawed her way up to a lofty status, he saw in Susan a genuine love of her work. Susan truly believed in her ambition to make the world a better place, and she was secure that her own niche in the world made a difference. Perhaps there was a glimmer of a chance for the two of them. There was so much of his past that he had held back from her—his career as a doctor and the horrible incident that had changed his life forever. Fear felt a rush of relief as he allowed himself the luxury of taking a chance on love. He would go to Susan. Tonight and together they would work out their differences.

''Fear, wake up, you're dreaming,'' Madeline called.

''I'm not dreaming,'' Fear said, leaping to his feet. ''But I have been asleep for too long.''

Fear reached around and drew his car keys out of

the desk drawer. ''Remember when I said I could baby-sit if you're stuck? Well, things have changed. I have other plans. I'm going to do something I should have done a long time ago.''

Madeline received his hasty kiss on her cheek and watched him walk out of the office, a happy man unused to happiness, with the shadow that had haunted him for years fading day by day.

Susan switched off the television, satisfied that the mild sunny weather was scheduled to hold for at least another week, thereby insuring an easier time at the challenge. The rock climb, she'd been assured, was little more than an exhilarating march up a steep cliff, yet the thought of rain-slicked paths was enough to put worry in her heart. The running race was no longer an obstacle, since Fear had gradually brought her to a level of competence where three miles was no big deal for her. Susan flopped back into the overstuffed cushion of her pastel yellow couch and wished again that she could have Fear with her on the weekend. Logically, she knew that the two-day event would pass quickly and that she'd be among friends and coworkers and have access to other contacts from the competing businesses.

The fitness challenge was set up to foster trust and communication within the company's upper management, and Susan decided that she should take advantage of such a good opportunity, have a little fun, and try to put Fear out of her mind. He had done the job she'd hired him for, and the signals she'd got from him—the admiring glances, the quick light touches, the fun of their time together—maybe that was how Fear Burns dealt with all his female clients. But Susan had seen him at Get Fit coolly deflecting feminine attention, and she knew that the way he treated her was special. Not that it made any difference now, she thought glumly, since the fun of the last few weeks would come to an abrupt end very shortly, now that she'd reached her goal and the final test was imminent.

The Tiffany lamp overhead cast a mellow glow in the room and she buried her bare feet in the plush carpet and yawned, wishing it were bedtime already. The past week had flown by in a haze of training sessions with Fear and early-morning runs, and although her body was fatigued, she was surprisingly alert and energetic on this, the last night before the team left for the lodge and the weekend competition. And not once in these past seven days had Fear shown even the remotest interest in accompanying her. Several times, Susan had been sure that he was about to ask if he could join her. He'd been so intent in his questions about her emotional well-being, and, regretfully, Susan had given no indication that she was plagued with doubts and insecurities that would vanish if Fear would only stay beside her during the long ordeal.

Why had she been so full of false bravado, when all she wanted was to have Fear there to speak words of encouragement, to push her past her doubts, and yes, even just to see the pride in his eyes when she excelled at the running race? It amazed her that she cared so much what he thought of her, but there was no denying the need she felt to win his admiration. Now, here it was the evening before the event, and she'd been unable to admit that she desperately needed Fear. Susan sighed and made her way to the pale yellow kitchen. Way up high in the buffed pine cupboards, a stash of forbidden junk food lay in case of an emergency.

This, Susan decided as she pulled a chair over to get to the cache, *is an emergency. If I can't have Fear, I might as well pack up a few old friends.*

Susan dropped the packages onto the bed next to the open suitcase, half-filled with sports outfits for the weekend away. A tiny flutter of guilt held her back from actually packing the goodies, and she frowned down at the jujubes and choco-chunk cookies, the super-deluxe bag of nachos and the sugary pop. Already, thanks to Fear, she was losing her childish love of snacks and realized the way she ate was primarily due to habit. Just as she was about to take the stash back to the shelves, a knock at the door stopped her. Susan glanced at her clock radio and then down at her flannel pajamas. Most likely it was Ingrid, a bit early, to give her a haircut before the big weekend. Ingrid knew how to trim bangs as precisely as a professional hairdresser and had promised to pop by this evening, a promise Susan eagerly clung to since she was suffering from a severe attack of nerves and knew Ingrid's calm good humor was just what she needed to put her back on an even keel. At least her dear friend would be there through the coming ordeals.

"Hold on a minute, Ingrid," Susan called as she crossed the small living room. Without a glance in the peephole, she threw open the door and caught her breath at the sight of Fear, lounging with one hand in his jeans pocket, the other clutched to Eire's collar. She felt her face go hot as his eyes lingered on her. Susan could detect a glimmer of amusement in Fear's casual greeting, and she flushed deeper when she spluttered a response.

Fear brushed past her and closed the door behind him. He shot the bolt and leaned against the wood, his muscular arms crossed over the white T-shirt. Eire whined and dropped to a sitting position.

"You really shouldn't open the door so trustingly, Susan," he said, his bushy brows furrowed. "Especially not when you're dressed like that." He spoke lightly but Susan sensed that he was indeed concerned for her safety.

"I usually don't get drop-in visitors at this time of night," she said. "And I was expecting Ingrid."

Susan crossed her arms over the flannel fabric of her pajama top, embarrassed at her silly outfit. She wondered if her hair was neat, but would not risk lifting a hand to smooth it down and have him think that she cared about her appearance. What must she look like to him, in the playful pajamas, rumpled and sleepy, her Miss Scarlet lipstick chewed off earlier as she packed up her hiking boots and sweatshirts and let the full reality of the weekend sink in?

If only she'd known that Fear was going to come over to her apartment, she would have showered and tidied up a bit and left the packing until tomorrow. Suddenly, she had a vision of her bed laden with bags of junk food and the door ajar. Her eyes widened in chagrin at the idea of Fear discovering the stash and assuming the worst, that she'd been cheating on her diet all along, when she'd been so good about eating healthily in the past few weeks.

"Aren't you going to ask me in?" Fear asked smoothly.

"You're already in. But let me get a robe," Susan said hurriedly, and whirled on her heel to rush across the room to shut the bedroom door before Fear caught sight of the incriminating evidence. But when she reached the bedroom door, he was right behind her, so close that he knocked into her when she turned to check his whereabouts. Facing him, Susan pulled the knob with her hands behind her back, and found herself caught between the door and his warm, powerful bulk.

"Don't tell me you've developed a Victorian modesty," Fear said, his dark eyes crinkled with amusement. ''Are you afraid that the mere sight of your flannel pajamas will drive me mad?''

Susan laughed nervously and moved to one side to pass by him, but Fear matched her move, blocking her passage once again, and she stopped and turned her face up to meet his serious face. He leaned forward, so close she could feel his warmth. She turned her face to one side, away from the man who stood so discomfortingly close.

''And how about your robe, Silver Sue?'' Fear murmured close to her ear.

''I don't need a robe,'' she said softly, casting a sidelong glance at his dark face.

''Really?'' he asked, and inched so close she could feel his breath on her neck. Susan jerked away from him and banged the door open.

''Don't go in there,'' she whispered.

Fear took pity on her wide-eyed, uptilted face and stepped back, yet that small respite was countered by his hands, which found hers and slowly rubbed the tender flesh there.

''But you feel cool, Susan. Get your robe and we'll have a cup of tea, like two old aunties up past their bedtime. Or we could have a drink, all right? Why are you looking at me like that? Did you have other plans tonight? Are you hiding something interesting behind that door?'' Fear asked with annoying persistence. His arms dropped to his side, and he craned his neck to see into the room behind her.

"No! Of course not," Susan said sharply, relieved that he'd at last given her some breathing room. "What would I be hiding? It's just that I don't need a robe." Susan took a deep breath and steeled herself to continue. "My room is a mess. A total jumble. I'm packing for the weekend, you know."

"For a woman as organized as you, I'm surprised your bedroom isn't a showroom out of a decorating magazine. The rest of the apartment is quite well furnished, if not a bit dusty."

"I have better things to do with my time than housework," Susan replied edgily. She put her hands on his chest and gently shoved him aside. "Now I'll make a pot of tea, if you don't think it's too late. Maybe you'd prefer a glass of red wine."

"Red wine, please."

Fear hunkered down on the striped sofa and put his feet up on her wrought-iron coffee table. Eire immediately curled up at his feet. *Such a cozy domestic picture,* Susan thought, as she readied a bottle and two glasses, *except his eyes are devouring me as he fixates on my every move, like a wolf in a herd of sheep.*

Susan deliberately sat as far away from him as possible, in the easy chair on the other side of the table. Fear took the bottle from her hand.

"Let me pour," he said, filling her glass to the brim. "And tell me, Silver Sue, what you're wearing this evening, would that be considered lingerie? Help out a poor ignorant man who had no sisters to straighten him out.''

''These are my most comfortable pajamas,'' Susan said. The first sip of wine warmed her to her toes, and she leaned back happily, ready to relax and enjoy Fear's presence.

Fear laughed and took her cue, visibly loosening up as she smiled across at him. He took a long drink, his eyes steady over the rim of the glass. Susan didn't look away. It amazed her how quickly her worries had vanished as soon as he sat down across from her, how delighted she was to see his face and hear his deep musical voice.

The cozy room held the two of them so naturally, with comforting intimacy, as if they were meant to be together, yet there was an undercurrent of possibilities that ran through the simplest conversation with Fear, an exciting hint of what could be. It dawned on Susan that she wanted to be with Fear, not just for tonight, but for every night from now until the sun no longer rose in the morning.

How happy she'd be to finally say what she'd been to afraid to admit. That disturbing, enchanting sensation that consumed her when she thought of Fear was love. She loved Fear. But it was never that easy. Her heart had made a decision without consulting her head, and Susan worried that her burning drive and time-consuming career would cause problems with the laid-back Fear. So many times he had made clear his contempt for working women. If only she knew why he was so adamant about family coming first, then maybe she'd have a chance to sort it out with him. But he held that part of him private, and that streak in him of sadness, of inscrutability, left her wary.

Susan broke the gaze and took a long drink of her wine. ''I hear all the rooms at River Gorge Lodge have a fireplace,'' she said, tucking her legs up underneath her. ''Can you imagine lying and watching the flames play out their colors?''

Fear set his wineglass down and sat up suddenly alert. At his feet, Eire caught the air of change from his master, and he too sat up and perked his ears at Susan.

''That's why I've come,'' Fear said in somber tones. His face was dark and unreadable, and Susan ached to reach over and smooth the furrowed brow.

''You've come to watch flames dance in my apartment?'' Susan said, trying to make a joke to relieve the sudden tension in the air. The teasing died on her lips as Fear pinned her with narrowed eyes, and she found herself holding her breath as she waited for him to speak.

''Listen to me, Susan. I know you're a strong, independent woman and there is no question in my mind that you can do this Corporate Challenge alone and without guidance. It's important to me that you understand I have the utmost faith in your abilities. You know I believe in you, don't you?''

Susan let her breath go in a long slow exhale and nodded guardedly, unsure in which direction Fear was headed.

''I realize,'' he continued, ''that my presence at the River Gorge Lodge is totally unnecessary, and no one has to point out that I won't fit in with the executives from the other teams at the cocktail parties and networking breakfasts. I know all this, but I would like to be with you this weekend.''

Finished with his speech, Fear slumped back against the plump pillows as if a great weight had been lifted from his shoulders, and Susan's heart went out to him. Hurriedly, before he spoke again, she moved to sit down beside him on the couch and took his large hand in both of hers.

''I'm so happy!'' Susan said.

''Then you'll agree to have me there?'' Fear asked, his face an adorable mixture of astonishment and joy.

''I've been wanting to ask you to come with me, but I never got up the nerve,'' Susan admitted. ''I was afraid that you would think I was afraid of the challenge, that I needed you to hold my hand and coddle me through the race.''

''Never! You're much too strong a woman, Susan. I knew all along I wanted to be there with you, if only to see you succeed where you once thought yourself hopeless. I knew from the moment I set eyes on you that you could do anything you wanted.'' Fear closed his large hand over both hers and stroked the soft skin with his thumbs.

"Thanks to you, Fear, I've never had half the confidence I appear to," Susan said shyly. "Even with my reputation as a top scholar, I was always terrified that I'd slip up, and I spent so many nights at my desk studying and rereading even when I really wanted to be out having fun. I don't know why I feel compelled to be the best at anything and everything. I suppose it goes back to being raised in such a competitive household and the fear that failure meant a withdrawal of affection. And I so wanted to reach my fitness goals with you. I didn't want to let you down."

Susan gazed deeply into his big brown eyes, astonished that she who considered any show of weakness to be intolerable was confessing secrets so deep she had never given voice to them until this night. Yet there was no embarrassment. Her words came naturally and left in their wake a quiet sense of relief to have shared these thoughts. Susan was sure Fear would think no less of her and suspected that he himself was on the brink of disclosing some of his darker past. When his strong arm circled her shoulder, Susan felt a security that had been lacking in her life, and she let her head fall against his chest and inhaled the wonderful fresh scent of his soapy skin.

"So we'll be together this weekend," Fear said, and kissed the top of her head. "Susan, if I've been mean to you, and I know a few times I've trained you too hard, I want you to know that I'm sorry. I'd do the same thing all over, of course, because look where it's gotten you, but that doesn't mean it was easy to force you. When I saw those big eyes of yours brim with tears of exhaustion, I felt like a complete heel.''

''I never cried!'' Susan challenged, her pointed chin raised in defiance.

Fear smiled indulgently. ''No, you never did, Silver Sue, and that strength in you almost broke my heart.''

Susan hesitated, then decided to ask the question that had been on the tip of her tongue in the past few weeks. ''You've had your heart broken before, haven't you, Fear?'' she asked as gently as she could. She felt Fear's muscles stiffen, and instinctively she rubbed her hand in deep soothing strokes across his broad chest, not daring to speak.

Finally Fear relaxed and took a deep breath. One hand found her silky hair and played with a strand. When Susan at last looked up, she saw no trace of misery in his expression; instead he smiled tenderly.

''If you'd asked me that question before I'd met you, I'd say that yes, my heart was damaged goods. But now I see that it was merely bruised.''

His arm tightened around her and he seemed to gain strength from her proximity.

''I was married back home in Ireland, when I was far too young to choose a direction in my life. I was content. Complacent, I would say, with all the indolence that that word implies. And when I wanted to start a family, the lady in question informed me that she had no intention of giving up a lucrative career to stay home with a passel of brats.''

"She didn't!'' Susan said, and sat up horrified at the callousness of someone who professed to love a man like Fear. "Is that why you feel so strongly about working women, because your ex-wife was so cold when she rejected you?''

Fear shrugged, his eyes hooded once again. "I just think any woman who has a choice is blind if she can't see what life is all about.''

Susan sat very still for a moment, weighing her response carefully. "I think a woman like your ex-wife was probably better off not having children,'' she said finally. "Other women are warm, caring mothers, even if they go out to pursue a career. Be fair and admit that one choice doesn't cancel the other.''

"The family suffers,'' Fear said with a shrug.

"But Fear! My own mother worked for my entire childhood, yet I never felt deprived. And my best friend and coworker Ingrid has the happiest children I know. You've got to see there's a way around the problems of a modern family.''

"Sure, and I do understand. It's just not my way to go,'' Fear said.

Susan frowned thoughtfully and took the wineglass Fear handed her. He obviously regretted having said as much as he did. Fear downed his own glass in one swoop and promptly filled it again.

''Would you like to talk about it?'' Susan asked.

''Nothing to talk about,'' Fear replied. His arm settled once again over her shoulder and he gave a tight-lipped smile. Susan sensed that his reluctance to delve into his past went beyond mere privacy into a realm of forbidden territory, and she delicately tried to steer the conversation back to his past.

''Do you miss Ireland?'' Susan asked.

''Not with my life as perfect as it is in this wonderful land of opportunity,'' Fear answered decisively. ''All my life I could never get enough running around. Some days when I was a schoolboy, I'd be tapping my feet at the end of the day, ready to run home and eat my fill, then go right back out again, sometimes taking a stack of bread and cheese out into the woods with me, so I didn't have to lose any precious time outdoors. And here I am, getting paid for doing the same thing, running around outside. I'm a lucky man, Silver Sue.''

Fear encircled her body with his other arm and drew her close. His arms were so strong that he half-lifted her from the couch with very little effort on his part and Susan abandoned herself to the heady pleasures of his kiss. Just when she thought she could not stand another moment of breathless dizziness, Fear pulled away and slid a trail of warm kisses down her cheek to her ear.

''You're wonderful! You are the most beautiful creature I have ever seen,'' Fear whispered. His kiss stilled any reply she might have had and Susan let her mind release the mundane thoughts and concerns of what this moment meant and let herself float. Far away she heard a door open and heard a warning growl from the dog on the carpet.

"Oh, look Mommy," a tiny voice called. "Auntie Sue is kissing a stranger!"

"Mommy, Mommy. Hurry and see the doggie," a second childish voice piped.

Susan and Fear dropped their arms and whirled to stare at the doorway where an overjoyed Eire wagged his tail at Ingrid and her two small children. Susan's hands shot up to her rumpled hair and she saw out of the corner of her eye Fear's hurried tug at his T-shirt. Susan opened her mouth but no words came out.

"I can come back later," Ingrid said, after she became aware of the two empty glasses on the coffee table, the soft lighting, and the flushed faces of the couple on the couch.

"No, no, come in," Susan said in a dazed voice. "Fear dropped in unexpectedly to give me a pep talk."

Ingrid raised her eyebrows and gave a skeptical smirk. "Is that what you call it nowadays?" she quipped. "Angie, don't pull the dog's ears!"

"Don't worry, Eire loves kids. And he adores having his ears pulled," Fear said as he rose from the couch and went over to tug Eire's ears straight up, like a rabbit's. "And you," Fear added as he pointed to the little boy. "What's your name?"

"Danny," the boys said, gazing up in open-mouthed wonder.

"You, Danny, are big enough to ride Eire and small enough not to squish him."

Fear scooped up the tiny child and held him over the dog's broad back. Patiently, Eire accepted the burden, and the boy shrieked with laughter and managed to hang on to the coarse fur for a few seconds before he slid giggling to the floor. Noticing the disappointment on the girl's face, Fear leaned way down and whispered a secret that put a smile on her face.

"Watch, Mommy. Look at me, Auntie Sue," Angie said, and crouched down beside the enormous mutt. "Shake a hand, Eire," Angie commanded, and an obedient Eire held out his paw.

"Play dead!" she said, and shot a worshipful look at Fear when the dog instantly obeyed.

Danny tugged at Fear's jeans and begged for another ride.

"I think they like you, Fear," Ingrid said drily, helping herself to an extra glass from the cupboard and pouring out the remainder of the wine. "Shall I open another bottle, Susan?"

"No, I want my bangs trimmed in a straight line," Susan said, now sitting cross-legged on the couch.

As she watched Fear goofing around with the children, she was vaguely aware of a new respect for the man stirring a chord deep within her. As he rolled around on the floor and took their blows with good-natured laughter, Susan knew that what she felt for Fear went beyond a mere infatuation with an interesting man. She simply could not imagine the rest of her life without him there. The very idea that love, true love, had snuck up on her carefully controlled life stunned her into numbness. She was oblivious to the surroundings as she stared straight ahead into the halo of light from the Tiffany lamp. *I, Susan Silver, am in love,* she thought. Instead of the elation the she hoped to feel, Susan sensed a looming dread that Fear might not feel the same.

Ingrid plunked down onto the couch and broke Susan's disturbing reverie. "Are you sure we're not interrupting?" Ingrid asked under her breath.

"You came in at exactly the right moment," Susan said. "Otherwise I might have made a fool of myself. Fear is very hard to resist." Both women looked over to where Fear lay flat on his back under a heap of dog and noisy children. His black hair stood up in unruly tufts and his cheeks under the tan showed pink from the exertion. The white T-shirt was hiked up, revealing a ridge of tight abdominal muscle, tanned to the same dark hue.

"So why resist?" Ingrid asked.

"Because he's not the right man for me, you know that. He's a jock and he will always be just a jock who works in a health club. Ingrid, I don't know what to do. I think I'm almost in love!''

Ingrid rolled her eyes heavenward and groaned. ''Susan, lighten up. You can't plan love as thoroughly as you plan the rest of your life. Can't you just let it happen? Go with the flow? Fear Burns may not be an intellectual, he might not have a burning ambition to run a multinational corporation, but he's what I would call a real man.''

Susan looked over to the kitchen, where the children stood waiting for Fear to pour them each a glass of juice. As she watched, Fear's eyes flashed up to meet hers, questioning, wary, and tinged with a darker passion. Susan caught her bottom lip in her teeth and dropped her eyes.

''What if he doesn't love me back?'' she whispered.

Ingrid took a moment to digest the fact that her friend was admitting to a vulnerability that was deep-seated, a fear driven by an overachieving family that was never satisfied with second best. Not only was Susan afraid of getting involved with a man her family would disapprove of, she was also terrified that this man would deem her unworthy. Ingrid took in Susan's wide, luminous eyes, her small, anxious features, and gently shook her head.

''Trust me, Susan, he already loves you. There are so few people you allow to see that human side and Fear has seen it and is still hanging around. He's here tonight, isn't he, and he wants to go with you this weekend. Give yourself a chance to fall in love. Forget all your well-laid plans and admit that you are not Superwoman, you're a normal woman with normal feelings.''

Susan glanced over at the kitchen and saw that it was empty. She leapt to her feet, scattering cushions. ''Where did everybody go?'' she said, and got her answer as the parade of children, dog, and Fear trailed out of her bedroom, each with armfuls of the junk food bags she had left beside her suitcase.

''Candy!'' Angie cried in delight.

''And chips, Mommy!'' Danny added, his voice muffled by the jumbo sack of nachos.

''And I've told them they can take it all home to your house, Ingrid,'' Fear said with a disgusted grimace at the bottle of pop in his hands.

''I won't allow them to have all that junk,'' Ingrid said. ''Come on, guys, you know the house rules.''

''Aw, come on, Mom,'' Angie said. ''Auntie Susan, make Mom change her mind.''

Susan, red-faced from being caught with the forbidden snacks, began to laugh, and soon Fear joined her.

''Old habits die hard,'' she said, when he laid his arm across her shoulders and squeezed to show her he understood the lapse.

''You won't need all that junk with me there. I'll keep you on the straight and narrow, Silver Sue.''

''Can we take it home?'' Danny asked, tugging Fear's pant leg.

''That's up to your mother,'' Fear said.

Ingrid tossed her braid and opened her mouth to decline, but Susan quickly blocked her.

''Of course Mommy will say yes, you may take the candy and chips, won't you Ingrid?'' Susan said with a wicked twinkle in her eye.

''But we don't eat like that at our house!'' Ingrid said.

''Lighten up, Ingrid,'' Susan said, echoing her friend's sentiments. ''Go with the flow and have a little party for the kids. Remember, rules are meant to be at least bent, if not broken and put out with the trash.''

Happily, Susan nestled into Fear's broad chest, and in a gesture more telling than words, circled his strong waist with her own delicate arm. ''If we're going to break some rules,'' she said, ''let's crack open some of that junk food right now and have a real party.''

A cheer rose from the children, and knowing he was beaten, Fear began to laugh.

''It's a good thing I'm going with you to River Gorge Lodge,'' he said, ''or there's no telling what you'd be up to out there.''

''Yes, Fear,'' Susan said, taking his hand. ''It's a good thing.''

Chapter Seven

River Gorge Lodge was an opulent resort built in the 1940s for a very wealthy clientele who wanted to experience the vast wilderness of the Canadian north without giving up the luxury of comfortable accommodations and gourmet food. Over the years, the lodge's reputation had grown and visitors came from all over the world to fish the pristine waters of the lake and hike the trails that snaked through rugged terrain to cliff-top vistas of enthralling beauty.

As she unpacked her suitcase, Susan found herself distracted by the view from her window, where the purplish hue of the mountain careened steeply into a lake that reflected the sun in a dazzling display of sparkles. The bed, she noted, was placed to maximize the view. Half-tempted to crawl under the puffy duvet and

130

shut her eyes for a few minutes, Susan instead went into the elegant bathroom and turned on the shower. Water shot out from a dozen points along the tiles and sent steam up to the high pine ceiling. With a sigh of pure contentment, Susan let her clothes drop to the floor and reveled in the warmth of soothing water against her skin. The trip had been far too long, culminating in the flight in the tiny Cessna airplane that took the team across endless green forests dotted with a hundred unexplored lakes. Just before the pontoon plane pulled up at the shore already replete with splendid private aircraft, Fear had pointed out a waterfall not too far from the lodge and promised to take her there with him tomorrow.

Susan leaned back against the warm tiles and let a jet of water massage her spine. Tomorrow was the day. All her training, her weeks of preparation and denial, would be put to the test tomorrow. Susan's confidence vacillated between extreme belief in her own abilities and sheer dread. The next morning, at eight o'clock, she would be racing along a wilderness trail as fast as she could propel herself for three miles.

Susan shut off the water and wrapped herself in the fluffy robe River Gorge Lodge had thoughtfully provided for all guests. *I should be happy,* she thought as she leaned her face against the cool window to watch the soothing rhythm of the waves down below. *I'm successful in my career, but I want more. I know Fear Burns is a wonderful man, but I'm worried about the future. Maybe I'm afraid of my own inadequacies,* she decided miserably. *Why else would I have never been in one good relationship, if not for my own hesitancy to commit? Why do I always let this fear of failure insinuate itself into my life?*

Reluctantly, Susan pulled on her shorts and the satin tank top with the company logo on the back. A volleyball match was the last way she wanted to spend the next few hours, but afterward, a buffet dinner was to be served on the terrace overlooking the gorge, and the thought of the dessert table cheered her immensely.

The opposing team in the fitness challenge was from a famous lumber company, and each member seemed to be at least six feet tall. The Silent Control team looked sharp in their shiny new volleyball uniforms, but Buzz and Natalie and Susan were dwarfed by the other players. As she faced her opponents through the net, Susan felt a knot of anxiety in the pit of her stomach. Susan clumsily flubbed most of her chances with the ball, flustered by the size of the audience in the bleachers. It seemed to her that at least a hundred pairs of eyes focused on her mistakes, and even Fear's shouts of encouragement did not console her. Although her teammates rallied and Calvin Hart served a perfect game, the opponents had several points' advantage. Bob, the president, gave her a consoling pat on the back as she flubbed yet another shot, and Susan felt her cheeks grow hot with shame. It appalled her that she was to blame for losing. She shot a searching look at Fear in the front bench, and saw his finger lightly touch his lips and point her way.

Instantly, her confidence returned, and as the ball flew over her head, she made a desperate leap to connect, instead sending it sideways as her small hand nicked the very edge. Ingrid moved in and spiked the ball down into the opponent's court, where a woman slid to save it and fell heavily to the floor.

"My leg!" The woman gasped, clutching her ankle. Her short dark hair fell away and exposed a pale face. The players circled around in concern.

"See if you can stand," someone said.

"No, that will make it worse," another exclaimed.

"It's likely just a sprain," Calvin said.

Fear appeared and knelt by the woman's side. His strong hand circled her ankle as the fingers of his other hand traveled up the back of her leg. "It's okay, I'm a doctor," Fear announced in response to the woman's frightened expression.

Susan was stunned. Fear Burns a doctor? How could she have spent weeks with this man and never know that he was a trained medical professional? Certainly, as she'd spent more and more time with Fear Burns she had discovered a sharp intelligence there and a spark of dedication that spoke of great inner resources not common to all. But a medical doctor! What on earth was a doctor doing running a health club and spending his evenings in pubs and nightclubs with his sports buddies?

Susan watched as the players lost interest and began to chat among themselves. Fear supported the injured woman as she hobbled over to the bench.

"So what do you think of our Dr. Fear?" Ingrid asked, at her side.

Susan looked up, dazed, and Ingrid punched her lightly on the arm.

"Wake up! How do you like that, Miss Intellectual?" Ingrid said with a mocking smile. "You're falling for a man who spent more years studying than you did."

"I don't believe it," Susan said, confused by the sense of betrayal she felt as she saw Fear apply a compress to the woman's leg. Susan crossed her arms over her chest and began to pace the gym floor. "He never told me," she muttered half to herself.

With a sharp whistle blast, the captain of the opposing team called the players to attention. "People! We'd like to call the game, due to injury. If there are no objections, of course."

Everyone nodded and murmured agreements except Calvin, who scowled. "I for one want to go on," he said. "I don't like to quit when I'm losing."

There was a moment of stunned silence at the blatant bad sportsmanship. From across the room, Fear jerked his head up and drew his bushy brows together.

"Oh, Calvin give it a rest," Susan snapped. "The

players are more important than the outcome of the game.''

Calvin's glare was almost comical, and Susan had to suppress a smile as he stormed out of the sports complex. As she turned to Ingrid, Susan saw, out of the corner of her eye, the president turn to his wife over by the bleachers, obviously upset.

''Oh boy,'' Susan whispered to Ingrid, her eyes wide and shiny. ''Now I've gone and done it. President Bob is annoyed at me for losing my temper. Any chance I had at the vice presidency is finished. And I came here to improve my chances.''

Ingrid looked slowly from her boss across the room to her little friend and thoughtfully shook her head. ''I don't think you've blown it, Susan,'' Ingrid said. ''In fact, I'd say that your outspokenness has clinched the deal. If anything, Bob is annoyed with Calvin Hart for losing his temper.''

Susan could hardly allow herself to believe Ingrid, so rattled was she by the rapid turn of events. ''I can't think straight,'' she said. One delicate hand lifted to her brow to rub the burgeoning ache away. All those digs she'd made to Fear about his dumb jock career choices—had he been laughing at her the whole time?

''My bet is you'll be the next vice president of Silent Controls,'' Ingrid said. ''And soon. If that's what you still want, of course.''

''Hush, now. Here comes Fear,'' Susan said, overwhelmed by the attack of nerves that hit her as Fear walked across the shiny floor toward her.

"Don't you mean *Dr.* Burns?" Ingrid teased. Seeing the stunned look on Susan's face, Ingrid quickly grabbed Susan's hand and gave it a comforting squeeze. "I'll leave you two alone," she said. "And I'll see you later at the buffet."

Already the big room was beginning to empty as the athletes moved on to the preparations for the evening's festivities. Now was the time to socialize, to network and exchange business cards over drinks in the main bar. But Susan's head was full of cobwebs and all she wanted to do was run back to her own little apartment and curl up on the couch with a bag of chips and a can of pop.

As Ingrid loped away, her familiar blond braid swinging with each step, Susan felt abandoned in strange territory as the enemy in the guise of Fear Burns's muscular form approached. He wore thin cotton pants that stretched across the bulk of his thighs, and the sleeves of his pale yellow golf shirt accented his hard biceps. This man was in better shape than anyone else in the room full of athletes. And probably smarter too.

Fear gave her his best pirate's grin and Susan found herself clenching her hands into small fists as she waited for him to speak.

"Good news!" Fear said. "The injured athlete was your only serious competition in the ladies' running race tomorrow morning. With her out, you'll be in first place for sure.''

Susan pressed her bowed lips together. ''That's no way for a doctor to talk about one of his patients,'' she said, her eyes flashing with hurt and anger.

''She's not seriously injured,'' Fear replied evenly. Tentatively, as if to gauge her mood, Fear dragged a finger over her chin and tapped her lightly.

''I would have told you soon that I was a doctor,'' he said.

''Really? Were you waiting until I criticized your lowly career choice again? Or maybe you're amused when I brag about my superior intellect. Have a few laughs at my expense.''

''No, it's not like that.''

''Fear, you're a medical doctor. I feel like such a fool treating you like a dumb jock and questioning your lack of ambition. A doctor's education takes years of discipline and hard work and a truly scientific mind. Compared to me, you're Einstein!''

''So who is comparing?'' Fear said harshly. ''Susan, life is not a test, can't you see that? You push yourself into these endless improvements with night school and qualifying exams, and for what? Who are you trying to impress? Are you impressed by my past career?''

''Well, yes, I am,'' Susan said reproachfully.

''So I was a doctor—does that mean it's okay to

get involved with me now? Do I meet with your cri-
teria now?''

Tears stung Susan's eyes. Surely he knew that he
already had her heart, long before the revelation of his
past. What had hurt her was the wall Fear had built to
keep her from such an important part of what had
shaped him as a man.

Susan crossed her arms over the satin tank top and
shifted her gaze away from his angry black eyes. Outside the sun sank lower over the cliffs, sending a
golden mellow hue over the treetops and the choppy
water below. The lump in her throat ached as she
swallowed and the words she had summoned to defend
her very nature died on her lips.

Suddenly, Fear grabbed her by her shoulders, his
large hands gripped the narrow bones, and he shook
her. ''Stop it! Stop doing that!''

''What am I doing?'' Susan breathed. Her luminous
eyes tilted up to his, her small mouth worked to keep
back the tears. Everything was going wrong—Fear
was angry with her, the president was not going to
select her for the coveted job, and she still had to get
up tomorrow and run three miles in front of all these
people. Susan blinked as her eyes filled and two tears
tumbled onto her cheeks.

''No, Susan, please don't cry, darling,'' Fear said,
and gently slid his hands around her back to cradle
her in his strong arms. Susan pressed her face into the
warmth of his shirt and felt the crisp chest hair below.

On the tip of her head, she felt Fear's lips nuzzling her hair and heard the comforting tone of his words.

''Come on, love. Don't let them see you cry.''

Susan pulled away from his grasp and straightened her backbone, her shoulders back and rigid. With the back of each hand she dashed away the dampness in her eyes and tilted her face up to Fear's. Once again, she was struck by how perfectly they fit together. If she lifted her chin one more inch and Fear lowered his own head just a small measure . . . she thought distractedly, her gaze focused on his finely etched lower lip. As if he read her mind, Fear raised his hands to the back of her head and buried his fingers in her glossy hair, pressing her toward him until his mouth found hers. His lips were hot and dry as he searched her own for the one spot that would wipe out her misery.

Feeling hungry for air, yet never wanting to break away from the rush of sensations his kiss brought, Susan let her head fall back away from his face. On her exposed throat, Fear left a trail of sweet kisses.

''We have to talk,'' he whispered huskily into her neck.

Susan nodded and took the hand he offered. Her shoes squeaked as they crossed the hardwood floor of the volleyball court. On the way past the bleachers, Fear grabbed Susan's warm-up jacket and held the heavy oak door open. The air outside was damp and humid and brought in the scent of ripe blossoms and fresh greenery. The golden sunset had deepened to rosy tones and Fear's features lit up with the soft light so his eyes gleamed with intensity. When the velvety lawn ended, Fear took the lead and led her down a well-worn path away from the lofty buildings of the main lodge. On either side of the trail, towering conifers and larches threw long shadows and sent up the pleasing aroma of pine when their footsteps crushed the carpet of needles that littered the earth. In one clearing, several log cabins built for guests of the lodge had already turned on the inside lights against the gathering dark.

The path forked at a rock face as steep and high as a three-story building, and Fear heeled right, to the higher ground, sure and steady as if he'd already been out exploring the wilderness.

Although Susan had no experience of the bush, she knew how easy it was to get lost in the endless acreage that made up the Canadian northern forests. But she trusted Fear with her life. Higher they climbed, until they came to a crest on a ridge where a stream bubbled across the rocky surface and fell over the edge in a frothing cascade that bounced off the strewn boulders onto the ledge below and streamed into the lake far down among the trees. The music of the waterfall enchanted them for a moment, and they stood hand in hand, perilously close to the brink, and watched the motion of the water. Fear's hand, at first on her shoulder, slid down to her waist and jerked her closer to him, so their hips were pressed close. Her head sank back against his shoulder and they stood for a moment in the stately silence as the darkness deepened in the sky above.

For an instant, they regarded each other, measuring the mood, and Susan lost herself in the glittery blackness of Fear's gaze. He must have seen an answering need in her own upturned face and roughly he pulled her against him. The kisses lasted as long as it took for the sun to finally dip below the cliff, sending a gray twilight to obscure the surrounding cliffs.

Fear broke the contact first. Breathing hard, he grabbed her upper arms and leaned her away from him. Susan saw in his swarthy face a question that hovered unspoken, and she hoped that he saw the answer there in her own eyes. Only when they walked back down the path in the gathering dark did she realize that neither of them had spoken a word.

When they got to the lodge, Fear took her past the disco bar where loud music thrummed and raucous laughter burst through the doorway and out into the grand hall. Susan felt immensely relieved that he understood her need to be alone with him, to talk without the distraction of other revelers in the nightclub. Susan needed calm reassurance that this emotion she felt was reciprocated. For him to truly open up to her, he would have to reveal something far more difficult for him to admit. She had to know why the sadness touched his soul and if that deeply etched scar on his psyche was going to end up hurting her as much as it hurt him. At this point, Susan would risk everything for this intense and all-encompassing love she felt for her dark-haired man. But niggling away in the back of her mind, a warning clamored in her logical, scientific inner voice. Susan ignored it.

Fear led her into the lounge area and sat her down on an overstuffed love seat set in front of a warm fire that burned brightly in the stone fireplace. The mantel stood as high as a man, and Susan's skin lit up in rosy hues that softened her features and glistened on her red lips. A stack of embroidered cushions invited her to curl up deeper into the comfort of the couch.

"Stay here and I'll get us some wine," Fear said. "Are you hungry?"

Susan shook her head and wrapped the warm-up jacket tighter around her. She wished she had taken time to change into a more appropriate outfit.

Fear set two tall glasses of ruby wine on the low table and sat down beside her. His hand rested on her leg and he smiled with such honest pleasure that Susan responded with a light kiss on his cheek.

"Susan, my love," he said softly, his kiss like the touch of a butterfly on her lips.

Susan took up her glass and nestled cozily into his shoulder, watching the flames dance. "Have you noticed how well we fit together?" she said dreamily.

"A perfect fit," Fear said, nuzzling her below her ear.

"When we walk together and you put your arm over my shoulders, it feels so right. There's no awkward spaces."

"And feel how perfectly your head snugs into my shoulder," Fear said, as he caressed her silky hair.

"A perfect fit," Susan murmured.

In the long silence a log in the fire crackled and slid noisily, sending a spray of embers up the chimney. Susan sneaked a glance at Fear's face and saw the dark eyes far away and tinged with the melancholy she longed to erase forever. But she couldn't help him if he refused to tell her what had so damaged him.

"Fear, I love you," she said. The words sent her heart racing.

His hand squeezed her into him. "And I love you so much," he replied.

Susan swallowed a big gulp of wine and asked the question she had to ask. "You seem so sad sometimes. I wonder, do you still think of your ex-wife?"

"Yes. But not in any way that makes me sad, and if you want to know do I still love her the answer is no. In fact, now that I see what love is, I realize I never really loved her at all. I was young and ready to be a man and I married the most glamorous woman I could find who also had a mind. Even as a young man I couldn't abide a woman without a mind of her own."

Fear gave a bitter laugh and squinted into the darting tongues of fire. ''As it turns out, she had no heart to balance the head.''

''She was a doctor too?'' Susan asked, her voice low.

''Yes, a brilliant surgeon who quickly turned to plastic surgery so she could travel in the illustrious social circles of film stars and supermodels. What a waste of a great talent!''

''Is that why you split up?''

''No. I would have put up with her gallivanting, but she shut me out of her life so completely when I wasn't interested in the parties and the gala events. We had it all, you see, money and success and fame, and I was foolish enough to think that my ex-wife would want to start a family. I never asked her to give up her career. I would even have compromised and hired a nanny, but Mary was not going to ruin her figure or her life with the mundane chore of child-rearing.''

Susan felt a scorch of anger emanate from the man beside her and his tone was one of disgust, but she sensed none of the profound melancholy he'd let her glimpse, not now, as he spoke of his past marriage. Whatever else he felt for Mary, it was not sadness or regret from a failed marriage. Susan was unsure of how far to press the issue. The surroundings were perfectly tuned for intimate disclosures. The lounge was empty but for a morose bartender at the entrance, the lights low, the only sound from the crackling fire and the occasional burst of laughter from the nightclub across the way.

Susan decided it was now or never. ''Fear, I wonder what happened to you over in Ireland to make you give up your medical career. I know you well enough now to see that you really care about people, and surely, that you're dedicated to the goals you set. And if you were a surgeon, that vocation is the ultimate in helping people.''

Fear turned to face her and locked his eyes on hers for so long that Susan began to grow restless. She broke first and looked away, busying herself with the napkin and the damp ring on the table.

''Someday I'll tell you,'' Fear said. He closed his hand over hers and stilled the motion. Susan's heart ached at the pain in his tone and she let her fingertips trace the black hairs that covered the back of his hand. Fear raised her hand and placed a delicate kiss on her palm.

''You make me happy, Silver Sue. I love the way you take on the world with that little chin of yours tilted up.''

''I expect to be challenged every step of the way,'' Susan said. ''All my life I've had to fight for recognition. Partly because of my size, I guess, everyone feels I must be coddled. Everyone except my parents, that is. Especially my father. It seemed that nothing I ever did was good enough for him. If I got ninety percent, he'd focus on what went wrong with the last ten percent. It seemed that because I had this super-intelligence I was judged more harshly than other kids my age.''

Fear ran his thumb along her frown lines and made Susan smile.

''Don't get me wrong. Dad was a wonderful man,'' Susan added, overcome by guilt. Her father had raised her and her sisters the only way he knew how, and it had paid off in three daughters who could support themselves in fulfilling, well-paid jobs. But at what price? she wondered to herself, only too aware of the deeply rooted fear she'd lived with, that failure would result in a withdrawal of affection.

''I'm sure he was, Susan, if he raised a woman like you. But I do see in you a burning desire to succeed, and that can be too much of a good thing. You're only human. Humans are allowed to make mistakes.''

Fleetingly the sadness crossed his features again, and Susan wondered just how much of his insight into acceptance of human error came from personal experience. Apparently there was some incident in Fear's past that had affected him deeply, and Susan longed to discover his secret and to comfort him. In spite of all the weeks they'd spent together, Susan was shyer tonight than she'd ever been with Fear.

''I guess I'd better turn in soon,'' she said with great reluctance.

''Your big race tomorrow. We'd better get you to bed right away.''

She lifted her arm and glanced at her watch. ''It's after midnight,'' she said.

Fear leapt to his feet and hauled her up from the couch. ''I'm still your coach,'' he said firmly, ''and you need some sleep.''

''All right, coach,'' Susan said, as they left the dimly lit lounge, hand in hand. ''Anything you say.''

''Anything?'' Fear said.

''Fear, you know what I mean.''

They stopped at the door to her room and he waited while Susan took the key from her warm-up jacket and unlocked it.

''You get some sleep, Susan. And try not to think about the race, all right?''

With a quick kiss, he was gone. Susan changed into her pajamas and fell into bed. Fortunately, she was able to empty her mind of all thoughts of the morning's competition, but the images that filled her head were far more disturbing. When she closed her eyes, she saw Fear's handsome face, and his wicked pirate smile taunted her in her dreams.

Chapter Eight

The sun's rays grew hotter as the morning marched toward noon, and Susan sighed contentedly and lowered her chaise longue a few notches until she faced the blue sky. The animal print of her sunglasses matched the trim of her white bikini. Tucked into her beach bag were a few magazines and pocketbooks that Ingrid had brought to the pool, but right now all she wanted to do was feel the deep heat on her body and revel in the knowledge of her triumph at the running race that morning. What surprised Susan most was how an event that she had been dreading for weeks had passed by so quickly that the details were a blur. All she remembered clearly was the sight of the finish line at the end of the forest path and Fear's tense expression as he spied her around the bend and raised

148

both arms in a mighty cheer. His presence had infused her with new spirit, just when she needed it most, and a burst of energy came out of nowhere and fueled her legs to pump ever faster. At the last instant, Susan edged out the leggy woman who had dogged her from the start.

A small, smug smile danced on Susan's lips as she recalled the flurry of congratulations and back-patting that followed her win. She was too keyed up to collapse right then, with everyone around, and only now were her muscles rebelling. Susan cracked her eyes open and watched the seagulls wheel in the cloudless sky over the cliff that dropped to the gorge below. The sun's heat drew an exotic piney aroma from the towering trees behind the pool enclosure. Susan wanted to stay right where she was all day, preferably with Fear by her side, and she didn't want to even think about the mountain climb scheduled for late this afternoon. The only way she could get up that mountain, she decided ruefully, was if her teammates tied a rope to her and hauled her each step of the way.

Ingrid emerged from the pool resplendent in a one-piece tank suit, and stood dripping onto Susan's legs.

''Yikes, that's cold, Ingrid,'' Susan said, drawing her legs up.

''You need to cool off! You'll get heatstroke baking in the sun like that,'' Ingrid said, taking the next chaise and topping her wet head with a baseball cap.

"Not me. I'm like a cat. I can never get too warm. Isn't this the most beautiful view in the world?"

"I can't believe my little Miss Twinkie won the race," Ingrid said proudly.

Susan shot her a pained look. "Let's retire that nickname, shall we? And you shouldn't be so surprised that I can win when I set my mind to it. Although it was a stroke of luck that the poor woman from the other corporate team twisted her tendons and had to pull out of the race."

"That poor woman has other compensations."

She followed Ingrid's look to the far side of the pool, where the poor woman in a teeny bikini and a bandage around her leg sat beside a very attentive Calvin Hart. Susan studied Calvin's perfect body and gleaming blond hair and wondered what she ever saw in him. How strange that she had been so devoted to logic that she had missed the fact that love couldn't be forced into manageable slots like some scientific experiment. Love fell out of the sky like a fallen star, hot and glowing and disruptive.

"I hope they find happiness," Susan said generously. "And Buzz and Natalie too," she added, inclining her head to the pool where the couple floated dreamily on a double air mattress.

"You are in a sweet mood this morning," Ingrid said shrewdly, "and I sense that the triumph at the running race is not the only reason for your aura. Have you and Fear worked things out?"

Susan took off her sunglasses, turned to face her friend, and propped her head on her crooked elbow. Even in the harsh chlorine water, Susan's hair had dried smooth and straight and swung out under her chin in a lively wave.

"Fear is the one," Susan said simply.

"You knew all along he was no dumb jock, but did you ever suspect he was a doctor? Why did he give up that kind of a career?"

Susan frowned worriedly as she remembered the torment in Fear's expression when he spoke of that part of his life. "Fear doesn't like to talk about that, but I know something awful must have happened back in Ireland. He's happy here, running Get Fit on his own terms. He's free now, in a way most of us can only dream of. That's part of what attracted me to him in the first place."

"And what about his distaste for women who choose a career over child-rearing? Have you worked that one out?"

Susan popped her sunglasses back on so Ingrid wouldn't see the anxiety her question provoked. No, they hadn't sorted out that part of their life yet, and Susan had not even brought the subject up, so afraid was she that Fear would stand rigid on this aspect that she herself felt so strongly about. Of course, she would give up her career if Fear insisted—she would do anything for Fear—but if she had to go that far, she knew in her heart she would never find a day's happiness again. So much of her sense of self was wrapped up in her vision of environmental research that if she gave it up for love there would be no replacing the satisfaction it brought her. But she would abandon that sense of purpose for Fear's sake. A life without Fear was inconceivable.

"I'm sure we can work it out," Susan said, her voice very soft. "Apparently his ex-wife refused to have kids so she could become a famous plastic surgeon. It's different between us. Fear knows I want children. I want *his* children. Surely he can understand that we can have a family while I continue my work."

"You don't sound too sure," Ingrid said, suddenly cold at the thought of her friend's despair if Fear refused to yield.

In the ensuing silence, a cloud passed over the sun and sent a long shadow over the pool area. Susan sat up and shivered and rubbed at the goose bumps that tingled up her arm.

"I'm sure," she said firmly.

Through the swinging door of the cabana, Fear stepped out, balancing a huge tray. On the table beneath the striped umbrella he spread out dainty sandwiches and fruit salad in individual crystal bowls heaped with fresh strawberries and ripe melon. Tall frosted glasses of lemonade dripped onto the white cloth.

Susan walked over and hugged Fear. "How did you know I was starving?" she said.

Fear's admiring gaze swept over her and he let her

go reluctantly. "You, my dear, are always ravenous," he said, "let alone after mastering the three-mile race course and being the first female at the Corporate Challenge to finish."

Ingrid took the cherry from the lemonade glass and popped it into her mouth. "What's so shameful about the win is that this pipsqueak beat *me*. My reputation as an athlete is shot!"

"She had the world's best trainer," Fear joked. His hand fell over Susan's in a gesture of possessiveness.

"Where have you been?" Susan asked. "I thought for sure you'd want a swim and a bit of relaxation. You are coming on the rock climb with me, aren't you?"

"I'll be with you every step," Fear said soothingly. "And I had to organize a few things this morning. See a few people."

Susan narrowed her eyes suspiciously. "That's a very vague account of your activities," she said. "What are you plotting?"

"You'll find out, my darling," Fear said. "Are your legs tired?"

Susan stretched her leg out under the table and groaned for emphasis. "My legs are like rubber. How I'm going to manage that mountain this afternoon, I don't know."

"I'll pull you from above," Ingrid said with a laugh.

"And I'll push you from below," Fear added with a wicked wiggle of his brows.

Susan's laugh was genuine and forced the last bit of concern from her thoughts. With the assistance of these good friends the climb seemed less daunting. Why, she was almost looking forward to the adventure.

Six hours later, Susan clung to a lofty rock face and prayed. In spite of her mounting terror and the immobility it brought, Susan gripped the cliff with trembling hands and felt strangely compelled to look below her. She simply *had* to look. Her heart caught in her throat and a small moan escaped as she saw far, far below the deeply etched river gorge where the river lapped the rocky banks and tossed logs that seemed as small as pencils. Birds circled the river, soaring beneath her. Dizziness hit, and Susan swayed backward and would have fallen but for the steady, strong hand against her lower back.

"Don't look down!" Fear yelled.

He stood on the rock ledge she had just climbed from. Fear had never lost his commanding tone of voice at each stage of this horrific climb. Part of her resented his lack of compassion in the face of her fear, yet she knew that without his bossiness, she would have given up long ago. Susan felt his hand close over her hiking boot and jam her foot into a space in the rock wall.

"Stop it!" she cried.

"Up. Push up!" he ordered.

Too numb to protest, Susan slid her hand up until she found a small grip and slid her body up. In that instant where she lost the pressure of Fear's hand, Susan panicked and looked down again. The deep chasm rushed up at her and the vertigo forced her to close her eyes. Then the reassuring pressure of Fear's grip returned and she felt her upper torso pushed up over the lip of the cliff and onto the level ground atop the overhang. Fear leaped effortlessly over the ledge and pulled her to her feet.

"It's over," he said, his voice kind as his hands rubbed some life back into her limbs. "You did it, Susan. One more triumph for you."

Susan regarded him mutely, her eyes wide with shock. Was it truly over? Surely she hadn't lived through the terror of the towering heights and reached the summit of that never-ending journey.

Fear took her cheeks between his hands and forced her face close to his. "Susan, are you all right? I'm sorry I had to yell at you, but it was the only way. I thought you were going to freeze. I've seen it before, with heights. I had to get through to you. Susan, speak to me, love."

All at once, Susan began to shiver uncontrollably and her legs turned to jelly. Fear half dragged her to a fallen tree warm from the sun, and sat her down, forcing her head between her knees. He stripped off his T-shirt and pulled the neckhole over her head. The shirt was warm from his flesh and smelled strongly of Fear's appealing scent, and Susan took comfort and sat up, gratefully accepting the water bottle he offered.

As she regained her equilibrium, Susan became aware of the deeply etched lines of worry on Fear's dark brow and she reached out and placed her small hand on his bare chest, tangling her fingers in the coarse black chest hairs.

"Thank you," she said.

"Are you sure you're okay?" Fear demanded, his arm locked over her shoulders.

"Yes, I'm fine. I think I'll be very happy that I accomplished this."

"You will be, I promise."

"I know. And I know that I never ever want to go rock-climbing again as long as I live."

Susan took stock of her body and realized that most of her fatigue stemmed from the extreme mental alertness the past two hours had required of her. Although her bare legs were scratched and dirty and her fingers were sore from gripping the rough rock, there was no permanent damage.

"And you forgive me for yelling at you?" Fear asked again.

Susan had never seen him so agitated. To console him, she smiled. "I needed it, Fear. Trust me, I'm fine. And I couldn't have done it without you."

"Are you absolutely sure? You're fine? Not suffering in any way?"

"Fear, please. I already told you," Susan said in exasperation. She leaned back into his arms and took a deep breath of the crisp, pine-scented air. Her reverie was rudely interrupted by Fear's leap upward.

"Let's go, then," he said, yanking her to her feet.

Susan tilted her face up to where he loomed, a powerful man ringed with sunlight like an icon. "Go?" she asked with a rigid smile. "Aren't we finished?"

"The finish line, Susan. Come on, on your feet. We'll be there in no time."

Three hours later Susan stood once again on the edge of the precipice, this time safely behind a guardrail and dressed in a clinging tulle cocktail dress, bathed and combed and complete with the Miss Scarlet lipstick to match her gown. It seemed like a dream to her now, those hours of climbing, and even though she had finished last of both teams, the mere fact that she had persevered and finished the nightmare climb at all was a source of great satisfaction to her. The president stood with her while his lively wife snapped a photograph.

"I'm so proud of you all." Sylvia beamed as she replaced the camera in her voluminous purse and took her drink back from her husband.

"Now we'll have photographic proof that we survived the climb," Bob said.

"Are we still ahead of the other team in the point standing?" Susan asked.

Bob's brows arched in surprise. "You know, I forgot to ask. Calvin Hart is the man to ask. He has an extremely competitive edge to his personality. It's these weekends that bring out character traits."

Was Susan imagining it, or did the president's words carry the hint of disapproval? The two men had seemed to be such arms-around-the-neck good buddies since the team arrived at the lodge on Friday that Susan had readied herself for the disappointment of being passed over in the selection of vice president of Silent Controls. She had almost convinced herself that the loss was all for the best, since she had the wonderful compensation of the new life with Fear. Still, at the thought of a second chance to advance herself, Susan's pulse quickened.

"Competition is a good way to test oneself," she said pointedly.

"Exactly," Bob said. "One's true character comes out in the fray of battle, doesn't it? You, for instance. You are such a tiny person, I'm sure that climb was a double challenge for you."

"It was hard," Susan admitted. "But I wouldn't trade that experience for an easier one. I feel really good about pushing myself."

Sylvia giggled and stroked her husband's arm. "Bob is so tall, he practically loped up that cliff. Why, at the end there, I thought he was going to win, until that Calvin Hart literally ran to the last trail and pushed his way up.''

''Now, Sylvia, he *is* the team captain,'' Bob said evenly. Still, Susan noticed that he frowned as he looked across the deck to where Calvin and the woman with the injured ankle snuggled on a wooden bench.

The night sky behind them was dappled with a thousand stars. Some couples were dancing but most were content to talk in low tones in small groups. Inside the glassed-in lounge, Fear and Ingrid shared a table to enjoy the sumptuous buffet table. Susan was not hungry. For her, the worst was over when she reached the summit of the cliff, yet the butterflies in her stomach persisted.

Bob stood beside her at the railing and leaned way out. ''Are you ready for the rough ride tomorrow?'' he asked.

''I'm looking forward to it,'' Susan said. ''I really have no fear of water.''

''Great to hear!'' Bob said. ''What a lot of fun I've had this weekend. Let's do the Challenge every year.''

This would be the final test, the results of her decision all those weeks ago to live up to her physical potential. So much had changed since that fateful day. So much more seemed at stake than surviving this one weekend.

''Let's get out of here,'' Fear's voice whispered in her ear. ''You don't mind if I steal your star athlete,'' Fear said more loudly to Bob and Sylvia.

"Just as long as you promise to bring her back for the rafting tomorrow," Bob said with a wink.

Susan found herself on a darkening path in the forest behind Fear as he moved quickly, dodging low branches and leaping over stray rocks. Her high heels sank into the earth and she began to pant as she tried to keep up.

"Fear, it's almost midnight. Where are we going?" she wailed to his back.

"Follow me and you'll see," he said, waiting with his hands on hips as she struggled toward him.

Susan balked as he caught her hand and tried to pull her onward. "Don't you think I've had quite enough exercise for one day?" she said as she glared up at him.

"Exercise is not what I have in mind," he said in a low voice. With new excitement, Susan followed Fear deeper into the forest. When they rounded a grove of ancient cedars, Susan saw a small log cabin, its windows lit golden by the interior lights.

"A house!" she exclaimed, hanging back. "This must be private property."

Fear laughed huskily and threw open the door.

"Very private, I hope," he said as she slid by him.

Inside a warm fire burned in a potbellied stove beside a king-sized sofa draped in a sparkling white quilt. On the table, an ice bucket held a bottle of champagne and two glasses. Beside the silver bucket lay a bag of marshmallows, two sharpened sticks, and a jar of chocolate sauce.

Susan whirled on Fear and took his hands to lead him in a merry dance on the sagging wooden floor. ''This is what you organized when you disappeared all day! And marshmallows—you know how I love marshmallows. And I haven't had them in so long. But you disapprove of marshmallows.''

''But I like chocolate sauce,'' he said. Fear took another step toward her, unwaveringly fixed on her red lips. A warm glow infused Susan from inside out as his mouth closed over hers and she let herself melt into the kiss.

''You're wonderful,'' she whispered as he pulled her down onto the thick blanket beside the fire.

''I wanted you to have an old-fashioned marshmallow roast, without the trouble of damp ground and mosquito swarms,'' Fear said. Expertly as a Boy Scout, he stuck the white puffs onto the stick and thrust it into the open door of the stove. ''You've been so wonderful about eating well and putting up with my commands. I know how hard it's been for you.''

''It has been difficult,'' Susan acknowledged, ''but I'm a better person for it. I know that now. I see how caught up I was in work and pursuits of the mind, at the expense of my physical self.''

Fear looked up quickly, his face suffused with hope. ''So you don't think your career is the main reason for your existence?'' he asked.

Susan saw the nuances in the shadowy dark eyes and weighed her answer carefully. "I believe that any material success is diminished without a love to share it with," she said.

Fear pressed his lips together and concentrated for a moment on the marshmallow. He pulled it out golden brown and handed it to her. "I believe that any material success is not diminished by lack of love; it is valueless. This should be the happiest time of my life, now with the success of my dream business. I'm rich from the profits. I get to set my own hours and live for my fitness programs. This lifestyle is what I dreamed about when I left the hospital back in Ireland."

"Did you leave medicine because of the divorce?" Susan asked, suddenly alert that the secret of his eternal sadness might be revealed.

"No!" Fear replied, scoffing at the idea. "I was well rid of Mary and her extravagant needs. I left for reasons far more serious than that."

Absently Fear took a fire log from the stack and added it to the flames. The fire roared to life and reflected red pools in his black eyes.

"Tell me, Fear," Susan said. Fear turned a mournful gaze to her and she saw once again the awful pain etched indelibly on his soul.

"I killed a child," he whispered.

Susan's heart lurched and plummeted to her feet. "No," she breathed, her hand over her mouth.

"As surely as if I'd taken the lad out and shot him,

I killed him.'' Fear stared into the flames, seeing once again the trusting little face of the boy, the shocked parents when he'd broken the news, the horrid inescapable headlines that pounded home his failure in black and white.

''It was heart surgery. My colleagues at the clinic had done the operation successfully before, but never on a child. It was at my insistence that we try. I knew in my heart that I could save the boy. I was adamant. It was my decision and I forced that family into seeing the surgery as the only way out. And I failed.''

Susan felt two trails of tears wet her cheeks as she saw Fear's shoulders slump.

''He died the next day. Two days short of his sixth birthday.''

An ash shot out of the stove and landed on Fear's arm. Absently, he brushed it away as if the pain had no affect on him. Susan knew no words of hers could assuage this deep-seated guilt, not now. To heal Fear would take a long steady course of love and careful words spoken at just the right time. It would take years, but Susan vowed she would release this man from his guilt.

''It wasn't your fault, Fear. Surely you have heard others say the same thing.''

Fear's face closed darkly, and only the fleeting image of raw pain remained behind his eyes. No wonder he'd had to throw up such a wall of protection if he felt the weight of a child's death on his shoulders.

"I assume all blame."

"You mustn't!"

"Why not? I forced those people to choose the operation. I practically promised them it would be a success. And I robbed them of their little boy."

Susan leaned forward and dug her fingers into Fear's arm. "All surgery is a gamble," she said firmly. "Those who select surgery know the risk. You were trying to help."

Ignoring her hand, Fear shrugged and busied himself with a marshmallow. "I didn't trust myself after that," he said, "so I got out of medicine and came over to Canada to start a new life. I don't like to talk about that time. As you can see, the memories are less than happy."

Susan chose to remain silent. He was hurt and he needed her, and she was sure that she was the one to bring her logical mind into the situation and fix the hurt. One step at a time, she would take the sadness from his soul and fill it with love and new memories.

In the stove, the marshmallow flared and instantly blackened. Fear pulled out the stick and dropped it onto his palm, cursing as the embers seared his skin.

"Now it's ruined," he said angrily.

"Nonsense!" Susan said lightly. "I like the black ones." She took it from his hand, bit into it, and savored the curious taste combination of burnt sugar and champagne. Her eyes closed as the stresses of the day and the revelations by the fire caught up to her. Fear slid his hand up her back and massaged her tired flesh.

"You are so beautiful, Susan, so delicate and finely made, but such strength lies inside. I am so very proud of you."

Susan allowed her eyes to close all the way. How wonderful it was to have someone you loved proud of you. Now if only he could learn to take pride in what heartened her the most—her fulfilling career in environmental research. Susan was so tired she couldn't think straight at the moment. She leaned back against the wall and tried to find a comfortable position, but the logs protruded in a half-circle and she had to slide to the floor just to rest her head. From far away, she heard Fear's husky laugh, so full of tenderness that even from the gates of sleep she wrenched a smile. Then strong arms circled her and she let her head sink onto his chest.

"You better go back to your room and get some sleep," he said.

"No, I want to talk. Tell me about your boyhood. I wish I'd known you as a child."

"After I walk you back."

Back in her room, she felt Fear settle her onto her bed and heard the deep rumble of his voice as he began to spin a tale. Soon the waves of sleep mingled with the words and drew her exhausted body down into slumber.

"Good night, Silver Sue."

Chapter Nine

Next morning, with the cheerful harangue of birds echoing from the treetops, Fear and Susan made their leisurely way down from their rooms toward the main lodge. Streaks of dawn still showed in the east and the sun burned through the morning mist with the promise of another hot day. Susan was eagerly anticipating the comfort of a booth in the breakfast room at the lodge. She felt giddy with elation. The world took on a new shape, as if all she saw was outlined in black and filled in with dynamic colors, and her heightened awareness let her hear as if for the first time the joy in the birdsongs.

This is what it feels like to be in love, Susan thought. *This is what the poets over the centuries have talked about, what I have been missing in my life.* She

166

squeezed Fear's hand and was rewarded with a warm pressure in return. When the lodge buildings came into sight, Susan felt the first stirrings of unease as the real world insinuated itself into her newfound heaven.

"Let's have breakfast," Fear said as they entered the main lodge and breathed in the aroma of coffee and bacon.

Susan took in Fear's stubbly unshaven face, his wrinkled white shirt, and the crisp hair that stuck up all over in little tufts. She smiled tenderly at his lack of vanity.

"Fear, I look a mess, but I'm starving."

Fear grabbed her by the waist and pulled her close. "You look ravishing!" he murmured into her hair. Susan arched her neck back, savoring the feel of his warm lips, and through half-closed eyes saw the president and his wife come through the doors of the dining room. She had to push Fear very hard to get him to release her. Quickly she ran her hands through her hair, tucked each wave behind her ears, and gave her most dazzling smile to the older couple.

"Good morning!"

"Good morning," Bob said. A mysterious smile played over his mouth.

"You two disappeared from the cocktail party without saying good-bye," Sylvia said.

"Did I miss anything?" Susan said anxiously.

"Not much. Unless you wanted to be a witness to

Calvin Hart and the woman with the ankle bandage dancing the Macarena,'' Sylvia said.

''And we have a new client,'' Bob added. ''The lumber company wants us to set up the computerized control system for their new plant.''

''Excellent!'' Susan said, her eyes bright with intelligence. ''Now I can control the noxious emissions right from the start. It's much trickier to retrofit,'' she added in Fear's direction. Suddenly she stopped talking. Fear's face was a complete blank. Was it from boredom or did it stem from the unfinished business of yesterday? ''Anyway, let's not talk business. Fear and I haven't had breakfast and we have to get ready for the white-water race this afternoon and pack up for the flight home.''

''Not so fast,'' Bob said with a laugh. ''I also received a fax last night.''

''You did? Way out here in the wilderness, still can't get away from the machines,'' Susan said ruefully.

''The fax was in reply to my earlier fax,'' Bob continued. Beside him, Sylvia nodded and beamed. All at once, Susan knew what he was going to say, and the knowledge bombarded her with a surge of delight mixed with fear. Motionless, as if she could make time stand still while she thought, Susan held her breath.

''Congratulations!'' Bob said, holding out his hand. ''You, Susan Silver, are the new vice president of Silent Controls.''

Susan's heart pounded wildly. She took his hand and shook it automatically, but her head turned back to Fear. With a sickening jolt, she saw that he was gone. In a haze of confusion, she whirled to find him, spinning in a circle taking in the golden wood, the hanging beams, the knots of people arriving for breakfast, but she could not see Fear. A lump formed in her stomach as her elation wilted into despair. She realized that her boss was waiting for some reaction from her and she forced a smile and shook her head to clear it.

"Wonderful," she said. "Thank you, Bob, for choosing me."

Even to her own ears, her voice seemed curiously flat for someone who had just received the promotion of a lifetime. How could the nice couple regarding her now with great puzzlement realize that her future had just shattered with the departure of the only man she had ever loved?

"Are you all right, dear?" Sylvia asked in concern.

To Susan's dismay, tears welled up in her eyes, and she looked down at her shoes and pretended to fuss with her hair.

"So, Susan, a new office for you," Bob said heartily. "We can discuss the details now, over coffee."

"I suspect Susan is overwhelmed right now," Syvlia said shrewdly. "Let's leave her to get through the rest of the fitness challenge without business intrusions."

Susan shot her boss's wife a grateful glance. "I am

a bit nervous about the white-water race this afternoon,'' she said.

''Nonsense!'' Bob said. ''You're a trouper. You'll
be fine. We're going to win this thing, and won't that
trophy look good in the front lobby of Silent
Controls!''

Susan excused herself and went back through the
double doors into the morning sunlight, hoping that
Fear was on the deck trying to find it in his heart to
be happy for her. If only he could see how much the
promotion meant to her, not just for the prestige the
title brought, or the huge salary increase, but for her
personally to be recognized and commended for the
innovations she had brought to the company. This was
no mere pat on the back—it was a chance to make a
difference in the world. Earlier she'd told Ingrid that
she would give it up for Fear's sake, but even now,
with the title so fresh, she understood that if Fear made
her choose, she would of course go with him, but there
would always be a lingering resentment like a wall
between them, right from the start of their time together. The deck was empty. A lot of the participants
from the challenge were still in bed, garnering strength
for the afternoon's event. Susan felt the sun on her
bare arms and closed her eyes for a moment as the
breeze cascaded down through the pines and gently
lifted her hair. Instinctively, she knew without a doubt
that Fear had gone into those woods to be alone. Her
eyes flew open and she set out on the hard-packed dirt

path that led from the bottom of the wooden stairs to the deep forests beyond. Whatever Fear had decided, surely when he saw her again, he would not be able to let her go.

Here in the shadowy pines the cool air was still damp with morning mist and Susan was cold and hungry and miserable. After she'd slid painfully on the loose rock that had fallen from the cliff above, Susan yanked off her shoes and stepped boldly back onto the winding path, only to be stuck with sharp pine needles on the soles of her feet. Hopping on one foot as she pulled the needles from the other, Susan heard a thunder of footfalls from above where the path wound out of sight. Her heart throbbed once and stood still.

Ingrid, out for her morning jog, raced around the corner, braids flying, and nearly knocked Susan off her feet. "What on earth are you doing here?" Ingrid gasped. "Are you lost? Susan, what is the matter?"

Susan threw back her head and let an anguished sob escape. Ingrid's comforting arm over her shoulders opened the floodgates of tears and she cried incoherently for several moments while Ingrid patted her back, like a mother with a distraught child.

Finally, Susan dried her eyes with the back of her hand and steadied her trembling lips. "He's left me. Fear's run off and left me." Saying the words, admitting the possibility of their truth aloud, purged Susan's grief and she pulled away from her friend ready to stand on her own.

''No! That can't be. You seemed so right together,'' Ingrid said.

Susan leaned over, clutching Ingrid's arm for support, and put on her shoes.

Slowly they walked back down the winding path. The trees thinned as they descended and the warmth of the sun came through in patches. The birds still sang but Susan's heart was heavy.

''I'm the new vice president,'' Susan said dully. ''Fear can't handle it, I guess.''

Ingrid knew enough not to congratulate her friend. ''You said from the start he resented all career women and had nothing but contempt for business,'' she said.

''Yes, I knew it all along. And I still let myself get hooked,'' Susan said.

''But you two seem so much in love!''

''I'm in love. I'm not sure about Fear,'' Susan said, barely registering the pain as her ankle wrenched once again in the stylish shoes. ''As soon as Bob told me this morning, Fear took off without a word. Last night was the most wonderful time of my life. I've never felt like that, and now it's gone. Over.''

''Maybe he's in his room,'' Ingrid said as the lodge came into view. The golden wood shone like a castle in the sun and a thin twirl of smoke rose from the massive stone chimney, sending the tantalizing scent of smoky pine into the clear air.

Susan shrugged and bit her lip. ''He's already made his decision. Now it's up to me. The only way I can salvage our relationship is if I catch him now and tell him that I'll pass up the promotion. I'm sure that if I have a regular job without too many demands on my time, Fear would accept that.''

Ingrid crossed her arms over her chest and frowned down. ''Do you know how lame you sound, Susan Silver? Remember for how long you coveted this new position? You're vice president, and if Fear loved you truly, then he would be proud of you.''

Susan shook her head. ''You don't understand. His past marriage fell apart because his wife let her career rule her. He's been hurt, and if he's oversensitive on this issue, I understand.''

''You are too good to be true. You understand his position. Let him understand yours. If he loved you, he'd let you move ahead.''

Susan headed wearily up the main steps, ready to continue the day and at least get through the rest of the fitness challenge before she could be truly alone in her little apartment to nurse her wounds and find a way to get Fear Burns out of her heart.

''It's not that easy, Ingrid. We can't escape what we are.''

Or who we love, she added under her breath.

Beside the group of humans clustered on the out-crop of rock, the river rushed by in a foaming froth of anger. Out in the water, huge boulders reared up in the middle of the cascade and sent up sprays of water that dampened the waiting group. Susan felt a chill creep over her exposed limbs. Compared to the surrounding forces of nature, Susan felt her own insignificance very strongly. Beside her the cliff rose above like a six-story wall and left shaded this side of the riverbank, but the water caught the light and sparkled in a torrent of liquid speed. The two seasoned river guides, one for each team, stood together and compared notes for the best start position for the rafts, which bobbed at the end of thick ropes ready to take on passengers. Buzz took a thick chunk of driftwood and dropped it into the swirling waters, and they watched as it raced across the river's surface fast as a bullet before it succumbed to the vicious whirlpool at the riverbend and disappeared.

"You look all goose bumps, Susan. Do you want my sweatshirt?" Ingrid asked.

"No, thank you," Susan said. "I don't want the extra weight if we turn over."

"Susan, the life preservers will keep us afloat. The guide said if we tip or get thrown out, we only have to relax and we'll float downstream to a calm pool."

"Didn't you see that stick that Calvin threw in?" Susan demanded, her eyes huge. "We might make it to the pool but first we'll be submerged for a few minutes and have our heads bashed against a few boulders. This helmet feels terribly inadequate."

Ingrid drew her friend away from the group and into the relative privacy of a clump of thimbleberry canes.

Through the thin-soled water shoes, Susan felt every pebble underfoot. Suddenly a great weariness came over her and she had no desire to continue. At first, it was her own driving ambition that had pushed her to explore the limits of her body in preparation for the challenge and then, she realized, after Fear had affected her, she had performed for him alone. Fear had drawn out the best in her by teaching her how to use those untapped resources, and Fear had been the reason she continued. Now the event was almost over and she had lost Fear.

After her foray into the woods, she had gone first to his room and knocked. She'd searched every nook of the club, knowing in her heart that Fear would seek solace in the outdoors, that it would be easy for him to scale the heights again. Maybe he'd even gone back to the cabin he'd so tenderly arranged for that one special evening, but Susan could not bring herself to face the emotions a repeat visit would bring if he were not there. Most likely Fear had left the River Gorge Lodge, never to be seen again. Susan swallowed the ache in her throat and decided to use her misery as a shield. She could be brave about climbing into that flimsy rubber raft, because at this moment she didn't care one bit what happened to her.

"It's Fear, isn't it?" Ingrid asked in quiet tones that were almost drowned out by the rushing river. "You're not afraid of the river. You love the water. You're still upset about Fear."

"I'll be upset about Fear for the rest of my life," Susan said, and despite her tiny size and the ridiculous straps of the helmet, her face held great dignity.

"Lovers' quarrel," Ingrid said simply. "You'll make up."

Susan chewed her bottom lip and considered the possibility that Fear was still at the lodge, walking in the wilderness, perhaps, and working out ways to stay together. Could it be true?

"Maybe you're right," Susan said. A glimmer of hope began to warm her from the inside out.

"You two love each other, and what more is there?" Ingrid asked, encouraged by the brightness returning slowly to Susan's eyes.

"You're right, Ingrid," Susan said. "I'm not giving up."

A great energy consumed her and she strode over beside the bobbing rafts and waited restlessly, jiggling from foot to foot until she received her puffy life vest and clambered into the raft. She settled against the rounded side and found the handgrip that was to keep her from being tossed into the raging river.

Ingrid and Calvin sat in the bow across from Buzz and Natalie, who for once seemed seriously cowed. Across from her Bob sat and grinned like a child at an amusement park. Susan was in a daze. Her co-workers were like strangers in the little cap helmets and puffy vests and Susan had the odd sensation of the world slowing down to dream time. The rough rises and dips of the tied-up raft seemed to hypnotize her into somnolence until the river guide yelled for their attention.

''People!'' she barked. ''I'm Helga and I will steer the raft. You must all help me by obeying instantly!''

Susan caught Ingrid's eye and both laughed nervously.

''This is a very serious course. We are not joking around,'' Helga said with a scowl to reinforce her words.

''And we're going to win,'' Calvin interrupted, his voice equally loud. ''We're ahead in the point standings and Silent Controls wants that trophy.''

''The tall man will please be quiet,'' Helga said. ''The most important thing for you as passengers is to stay seated.''

''I just want to stay in the raft,'' Bob said, his grin less wide now that the raft lurched beneath him.

''Keep on trucking!'' Buzz said with a rebel yell. Natalie giggled and splashed a handful of water his way.

''The big man will need to listen,'' Helga said sternly. ''This is serious business. Now listen for the whistle and we will be released.''

On shore, two staff members knelt by the ropes, ready to release at the sound of the whistle. Susan searched the shore anxiously hoping for a last-minute show but Fear was noticeably absent. In the next raft, the opponents waited in silence.

The whistle died and left in its wake the screech of

circling gulls overhead. In an instant, the raft left the gulls far behind as the current ripped them from the bank and pitched the group headlong into the very center of the river. Susan's breath caught as the two rafts raced for the narrow white water between two boulders.

Suddenly the other raft turned backward and careened off course, allowing the Silent Control raft to shoot through the opening unchallenged. A cheer rose from the team and Susan felt a rush of adrenaline as the raft slowed dramatically and then was tugged by an underlying current and raced once more into the spray of water. Behind them, as they reached the curve in the water, the other raft had caught a subcurrent and picked up speed.

''Hurry!'' Susan shrieked joyfully and dug her paddle into the froth.

''Paddle!'' the guide yelled.

Laughing, her face drenched, Ingrid turned from the bow and gave Susan the thumbs-up.

Susan threw back her head and inhaled the fresh damp air. The raft dipped and slammed down a small waterfall and she gripped the handle and waited to get her balance again. Fortunately, the river straightened out for a bit in a smooth expanse where the cliffs rose less steeply on the far shore and the trees reflected in the water gave a deep green hue to its depths. Susan relaxed enough to look around, not even admitting to herself what she was searching for. Then her heart leaped. For there on the low rocky ledge just ahead of the raft sat a familiar figure. The sun glinted on Fear's crisp black hair and threw shadows on his bare chest, so it seemed that he stood larger than life. Susan's elation soared to new heights. The world had reached a state of perfection that filled her with unprecedented joy and she waved her paddle high in the air.

"Fear! Fear!" she cried.

"Stop rocking the boat!" Ingrid screamed.

"Don't panic!" Helga ordered.

"Fear!" Susan called, turning as they passed his outcrop. "I love it! I love you!"

"Get that kid to settle down," Helga barked.

"That's not a kid. That's our research scientist," Ingrid shouted.

"That's our vice president," Bob corrected.

"Watch out!" the guide shrieked.

The raft caught a swirling eddy, hung on the edge for a second, and spun sharply to the right. In a split second, Susan flew out of the raft and into the deep water. Spluttering and instantly alert, she bobbed to the surface in time to see the raft disappear around a clump of rocks. On the edge of panic, Susan looked back to where Fear had been, only to find that the river had swept her away from that point, so rapidly she was disoriented and breathless from her sudden plunge. When she tried to take a deep breath, the river had other ideas and pulled her from below, feet first, into the white angry foam that had only moments before been smooth water. Susan felt her body being torn in different directions and she winced as her leg scraped over a hidden rock. When she tried to swim against the current, the river tossed her like a doll away from her goal. The water was icy. Soon her muscles, already tested to their limit, grew weak with fatigue. The last thing Susan saw was a sharp-edged boulder rushing toward her and then the blue sky spinning into blackness.

The first pain jabbed up sharply from her ribs as she became aware of her own ragged breath. Then the throbbing beat of an ache joined the chorus of pain in her head and Susan kept her eyes closed as she lay motionless on sweet solid ground, as still as possible to keep the pain from overwhelming her. While she managed through sheer force of will to banish her physical hurts from the center of her thoughts, the heavy weight of Fear's sudden loss washed over her and filled her heart with agony. Had it really been Fear up on those cliffs? She was sure of it. A woman knew her man from any distance from the small details only she would notice—the shape of his head outlined against the sky, the faint slope of his powerful shoulders. It was him. She knew it. Yet maybe he had come to watch the end of the fitness challenge strictly from a professional sense of duty. Or out of mere curiosity. Fear had already made it clear that he had no intention of sticking around. If only she could talk to him and make him realize what she would sacrifice to keep him in her life! Her body, sore as it was, would heal, she knew that, but her heart would be forever damaged without her Fear. A moan escaped her lips.

''Hush, now, darling,'' a voice said.

Slowly she became aware that her upper body rested against a warm lap and she felt a soothing hand on her temple. Strong fingers circled her wrist. Susan opened her eyes a slit and let her fuzzy vision take in a wrist, a muscled ropy arm, then the face bent over her—a dear, handsome face, his black eyes crinkled with concern. Fear's tawny skin held two blotches of red over his hard cheekbones and his hair stuck up in damp tufts. He was all wet!

''Fear!'' Susan breathed weakly. ''You didn't leave me.''

She heard a sharp expulsion of air, as if Fear had held his breath until he saw her fully conscious and out of danger.

''I'll never leave you, Susan,'' he said, his tones husky with emotion. Both his hands cupped her face and he locked his eyes onto hers. ''I thought I'd lost you. When you pitched into that river, you went under for such a long time. Oh, Susan, I was terrified.''

''You were?'' she said weakly.

''I was halfway down the cliff before you surfaced. You looked so small in that raging river, so helpless. I knew right then that if anything happened to you, I couldn't go on.'' He stopped, too choked with remembrance to continue. Susan lifted her hand and let her fingers rest on his cheek. His skin felt very warm.

"I love you, Fear," she said, trying to summon a smile. "I want to tell you something important. I can't live without you either, and I want to give up my promotion to make you happy."

"But then you won't be happy. I've decided that your happiness is more important to me than anything in the world. Can't you see that you could have died this afternoon? And then where would I be, bereft of your sweet presence in my life?"

"Do you mean that?" Susan asked.

"Yes. When a near-tragedy strikes, all the petty problems get put into perspective. We're meant to be together."

"But all the things you said," Susan murmured. Her hand found the ache on her forehead and rubbed. Gently Fear lowered her hand and replaced it with his own.

"Are you in pain, Susan?"

"No. Not anymore," she said. "But Fear, I want to make you happy. I know that sadness in you and I want to make it better."

Fear shook his head. "Can't you see that you've already made it better? Silver Sue, for a smart woman, you can be very dense sometimes. This accident could have been another loss in my life. Instead it's a gift."

"A gift!" Susan said, struggling to sit up.

"Yes! I've learned a lesson about what is important.

I want you to be my wife, to share my life, and that's what is real. The details are trivial.''

''But I'm willing to give up my promotion. I can still be content with my research if I have you. My life has no meaning without you.'' Susan felt hot tears well up behind her lids and she clenched them shut, dizzy with the delayed shock of her ordeal.

''Don't talk now,'' Fear said softly. ''Please. Let's enjoy this second chance. Let's just be together.''

With great tenderness, he laid a silencing finger over her cherry red lips and tapped gently. Susan caught the tip of his finger between her lips and kissed the hard skin. Fear's sharp eyes swept her up and down as if assessing her state of well-being, and satisfied, he swept her up into his arms, half kneeling as she lay propped up from the hips. So strong was he that she sagged back in his embrace fully supported as his lips met hers. Never before had she felt this safe. His kiss filled her battered body with a healing heat and she slid her hands over the the line of rippling muscles along his back, savoring the shape and form as he moved to caress her. As she responded to his tender kisses, Susan let herself drift while the world around her disappeared.

''Stand back!'' a voice commanded.

Fear gripped her and they both jerked their heads around to face two paramedics wielding portable life-support machines.

''We'll take over the CPR now. Lie down, Miss.''

Susan gaped at the oxygen mask the man was lowering toward her face.

The second paramedic made a grab for her wrist. ''Pulse high! Very high,'' the man barked.

Susan looked over at Fear's astonished face and began to laugh. She batted feebly at the plastic mask and shook her head to ward it off. Fear leapt to his feet and drew a heavy hand over his chin as he tried to regain his equilibrium.

''I know how this looks,'' he began.

The two uniformed men pulled away from their attentions to Susan and frowned at him suspiciously. ''This is the victim?'' the younger paramedic asked, unsurely.

''Yes. I mean no. She's fine. Stand up, Susan. Show them just how fine you are.''

Susan stood up, grinning at the bizarre situation, and took the hand that Fear held out for her. ''I'm fine.''

The two paramedics were reluctant to relinquish the drama, but there was no denying the healthy blush on Susan's face, the apparent ease with which she sprang to her feet.

''We have to check her out,'' the older man grumbled. ''Rules are rules.''

''You *are* the girl who fell in?'' the younger one said. ''Apparently, someone jumped in out of nowhere and fished you out of the water. It could have been a drowning, because even life preservers can't save you if you're floating facedown.''

"For insurance purposes, we have to examine her," the senior paramedic said. "We were officially dispatched from the first-aid station at the lodge."

"She might have lung damage," the second man said.

"Or a skull fracture," the other said.

Fear dropped Susan's hand and crossed his arms over his powerful chest. "I'm Dr. Feargal Burns, and I can assure you that my patient has no hematomae, abrasions, or contusions. A mild concussion, yes, but we were interrupted before I could thoroughly examine the young lady." Susan's giggle escaped from behind her hand as the two medics shrank away from Fear's authoritative manner. "In fact, if you would allow us some privacy, I could continue my appraisal and confirm my initial findings. Shall I send you a full report? In triplicate?"

The senior paramedic looked from Fear's intimidating form to Susan's slight and trembling figure and began to put the scene in a different light. Suddenly, he grinned.

"Aha! I understand now, Dr. Burns. Of course, she'll need round-the-clock observation," he said with a wink.

"My pleasure," Fear replied.

"I could stay with her," the younger man piped up, earning a hearty shove from his superior.

"Let's get out of here. Dr. Burns will set things

right. We'll report back to base, let the teams know she's all right.''

As the two medics climbed away up the cliff, Fear led Susan farther away from the rocky shore and up behind a fallen tree where the thunder of the river was dulled by the leafy branches.

"Susan," he said and put his hands on her hips. Susan circled his neck with her own arms and tipped her face up. What she saw in his eyes filled her with wonder, for there in the depths of the spiraling blackness, she saw that at last the terrible sadness had been banished. Not a trace remained to taint the true love she saw reflected there. Her eyes misted with tears and yet her mouth curved up in a smile.

"Fear, I owe my life to you," she said.

"I'll take that life and join it to mine, if you accept," he said.

"I do. I love you. We'll work it out, won't we, if we truly love each other?"

"Yes," Fear said, smiling back.

"You rescued me," she whispered as he pressed his forehead down against hers and she drank in the warm, familiar scent of him.

"No, my love," Fear said. "In the way that truly counts, you rescued me."

Below their small haven, the river flowed in a winding course as old as time. Like love, it set its own course, and like love, it somehow seemed to know just where to go.